My Sister Sif

Ruth Park
My Sister Sif

Viking

VIKING
Published by the Penguin Group
Viking Penguin, a division of Penguin Books USA Inc.,
375 Hudson Street, New York, New York 10010, U.S.A.
Penguin Books Ltd, 27 Wrights Lane, London W8 5TZ, England
Penguin Books Australia Ltd, Ringwood, Victoria, Australia
Penguin Books Canada Ltd, 2801 John Street, Markham, Ontario, Canada L3R 1B4
Penguin Books (N.Z.) Ltd, 182–190 Wairau Road, Auckland 10, New Zealand

Penguin Books Ltd, Registered Offices: Harmondsworth, Middlesex, England

First published in Australia by Viking Kestrel, 1986
First American edition published in 1991

1 3 5 7 9 10 8 6 4 2

Copyright © Kemalde Pty Ltd, 1986
All rights reserved
Library of Congress Catalog Card Number: 90-50999
ISBN 0-670-83924-8
Printed in the U.S.A.
Set in 12 point Sabon

J PARK

Chapter 1

These things happened when I was fourteen years old. At that time my sister Sif was seventeen. I have a photograph of her as she was then, gentle-eyed, her hair blowing around like black cobweb.

My sister did not often smile and rarely spoke. Yet most of the words I remember from my childhood were said to me by Sif.

'Erika, don't hurt that caterpillar. It means to be a butterfly some day. Erika, inside that peach stone is a tree, folded a million times. So go and plant it.'

And, most often: 'Erika, Joanne doesn't intend to be mean to us. It's just that she's frightened.'

Joanne was our elder sister with whom we lived in Lindfield, a Sydney suburb. She had a chilly house and chilly ways. She was married to James Bowman, a polite man much older than herself. Their children were Giselle, aged two, and Travis, an edgy, lying little boy of six.

When our father Erik Magnus died, Joanne became our guardian. She did not welcome the responsibility.

Sif scolded me when I said Joanne must have been adopted.

'You don't understand her,' she said. 'Joanne worries because our family is different. She thinks the difference may spoil the life she's made for herself.'

'She's always putting us down,' I said. 'You especially.'

1

'I remind her,' said Sif.

We Magnus children were born on an outer island of the Epiphany Group in the Pacific Ocean. This island is called Rongo, and it is so small no one in the world cares about it except the people who live there. It is just above the Tropic of Capricorn, lying halfway between the Friendlies and the Cook Islands, south-west of Tahiti and the Marquesas.

One night many years ago, our father, a Scandinavian seaman, jumped from his ship and swam two kilometres to Rongo. He could see it upon the glittering horizon, a black citadel. Humpback whales and dolphins swam with him, the whales mute, the dolphins creaking and whistling encouragingly. They are always anxious about humans swimming in deep water. In this experience of Father's began — except for Joanne — our family's love for sea beasts.

The Polynesian people who live on Rongo, idle and carefree, welcomed our father and soon considered him one of themselves. He married a girl called Matira.

Father led a happy life. At that time there was only one other white man on Rongo. Dockie had once been medical officer on the Big Island of the Epiphanies. He was kind and wise and had read every book in the world, I think. He educated all of us when we were young. He was, however, a drunkard, and our father very soon became one as well. These two friends opened a general store and, drunk or not, managed to keep it open and make enough money to send us girls to boarding school in Sydney.

Joanne never returned to the Island, never once. She spent the holidays with school friends. But Sif and I travelled back every year. We were there when Father died. He had the same sea-blue eyes as Sif and his hair had been dark in his youth. His tall body, strong as a castle, was now a crumbling castle. He said that Joanne was to look after us while we were young.

'But Father, she doesn't like our world! She even hates our names. She calls herself Joanne instead of Johanna, and Sif Sarah, and me Erika, though I don't mind that so much. She wants to forget about Rongo and Mother and everything.'

'You have a long tongue, little girl,' said Father, sighing.

He made Sif and me promise to obey Joanne and not go against her judgment unless it were for a serious reason. Even though I was only ten I knew I was locking myself into a prison.

'Pour me some schnapps,' said Father, but he was too feeble to drink it.

Because of that promise we were now in the hands of Joanne. To make matters worse, for some reason of her own she removed us from boarding school. We were now day pupils, and so we were always under her feet. Our sister's impatience broke like a sullen sea over Sif. Nothing she did was right. Before Joanne's reproaches she fell into defenceless silence.

'What's the matter with you, Sarah? Answer when I speak to you!'

'Sarah doesn't know what to say,' I ventured timidly. Long before, I had realised that the person Joanne would notice and bully least was an obedient little mouse. This I had become. I don't think she ever wondered why a girl as smart as I was at school could be so fluttery and dumb within the Bowman household.

'You don't know what to say about your own future!' fretted Joanne. 'You've messed up your education; you'll never get into University now. I believe you're too dopey even to do a secretarial course.'

'Here, hold on, Jo,' interrupted James. He was always upset when she badgered Sif.

But it was true that Sif had done shamefully in college. Joanne said she was just lazy, but the truth was that the city was a torment to Sif. She was stupefied by its grinding noise, the tainted air, the people — millions of people rushing, crushing, not looking at one another or the sky. Sif could not adapt to the city because she never would be of the city.

Her wretchedness got in the way of her sleeping or eating properly. She always seemed to have a cold.

'Perhaps she could train in hairdressing,' suggested James kindly.

'Don't make me be a hairdresser,' whispered Sif, looking as if he'd advised that she should be a murderer.

'You're seventeen, Sarah,' cried Joanne. 'What *do* you want to do?'

'I want to go home,' said Sif almost inaudibly. Her thin hands trembled.

'Of course you can't go back to that dead and alive hole,' Joanne exploded. 'Have some sense. What would you do there? Lie around on the beach and get fat like the Islanders? Take to the bottle like Father?'

'Rongo isn't a hole,' said Sif. 'It's perfect.'

Joanne went off into some rattle about wasting the money Father had left for our professional training, and hopeless idiots who didn't know enough to come in out of the rain. In his nice way James endeavoured to interrupt the flow. I could see Sif did not hear a word. In her mind she was looking at our Island, perhaps as it was from the sea — a spine of black bone, its wrinkles green with hanging forest, its hollows inhabited by cloud. Or maybe from the air, the reef mapped in ghostly meadows of green and butterfly blue.

4

In bed that night Sif said mournfully: 'I don't want to make Joanne angry with me. But I don't know how to be any other way.'

I knew she was especially homesick because in a few weeks it would be June. June was an important month on Rongo. It was then the whales came back to the Epiphanies.

Under the demureness I had cultivated in order to be able to bear Joanne and her house, there was a fierce crafty spirit, at least where Sif's welfare was concerned. The light shone out of her for me. I was a were-cat. When Joanne tried to make Sif into somebody she was not I could have scratched her eyes out.

'Sif,' I said 'you have to go home. I've been thinking about it. We'll run away.'

'But how? We haven't any money. And it takes a lot of money.'

'We have the shells.'

Each time we had returned to school after the holidays we had brought shells to remind us of Rongo. Some were huge and sumptuous — bailers, spider shells and tritons. I exchanged many of these for books and other treasures.

Since I had come to think that we might run away, I had studied books on shells. Most of those we had were of little commercial value. There were, however, two harp shells, which I had saved because of their freakish colour. Harp shells are small, with raised glossy ribs freckled with black. The shells are coloured variously from grey to a plummy brown.

Those I had found on the outer reef at Rongo were red. The inner lip, polished like silk, was as dark as rubies. They were, in fact, that rare shell, the ruby harp. I was excited when I saw in the books photographs of some of the thirty or so ruby harps ever found. Being practical, I rang up a shell dealer in the city, asking him prettily for approximate shell values for a school project I was doing. He laughed when I mentioned ruby harps, saying he'd seen only three in his lifetime.

'Yes, but please, what would they sell for?'

The sum he mentioned failed by fifty dollars to cover the cost of two airfares to Rongo, one return. So I had some facts to give my sister. She turned very pale and pulled up the blanket as if she wanted to hide.

'Oh, Erika, we wouldn't dare. Joanne would go out of her mind. She'd have us brought back.'

'You're wrong, Sif. She'd make a frightful commotion, and then when she thought about it she'd be glad. You go first and borrow the fifty dollars from Dockie and send it to me and I'll slip away and follow you. I don't want to miss term exams.'

I had worked it all out. Because of past holidays, our passports were in order, and there would be no trouble getting our flight tickets. We would take Mr Califano of the fruit market into our confidence. He didn't like Joanne; she had been snappy with him and hurt his feelings. Sif could send the fifty dollars care of Mr Califano's shop.

'Stop fussing, Sif,' I begged. 'When she starts yelling I'll just tell her that you've gone home to Rongo and aren't coming back. She won't dream that I'm going too. Well, come on, what about it?'

Sif still looked like a ghost.

'Father said we had to obey Joanne. We promised.'

'Unless there's a serious reason,' I reminded her. 'And there is. The city doesn't suit you, you're all eyes and bones, and you've had that cough for weeks. If you stay here, well, I don't know what might happen to you.'

6

'James has been really kind to us,' she said.

She went on with this so long that at last I hissed: 'Oh, shut up! You can't see beyond the end of your nose.'

I thumped over on my side and went to sleep. The next morning I said curtly: 'If you can't make up your mind, I can! I found those shells and I'm going to sell them today.'

'You're mad with me,' said Sif sadly.

'I'm boiling mad,' I said. 'We've only this one chance to get away. How could we ever earn enough money? Not for years! And you sit there dithering. I've no patience. Sometimes I think you *are* Sarah. Something ·Joanne's made up.'

I went off, not to school, but into the city.

The shell shop owner loved his wares, you could see that. The shop was clean and the shells glistened. There was a faint smell of ocean which I breathed with pleasure. The man gave me that look all shopkeepers direct at children — wariness in case I knocked something over and vexation because I would likely waste his time. I went straight up to him and said, 'I have two ruby harps. Are you interested in buying them?'

He was sharp. He asked: 'Are you the girl who phoned me a week or so ago?'

'Yes,' I said. 'I collect shells.'

By this time I had the ruby harps out of my case. In case he tried to bluff me I had brought along my shell books as well. I put them on the counter so he'd see I wasn't just an ignorant schoolgirl. But there was no need. The moment I slipped the ruby harps out of their tissue and on to the black velvet tray his face told the story. He didn't even try to hide his eagerness.

'Very fine specimens,' he said. 'How did you get hold of them?'

'Found them.'

'In Australia?'

'No.'

It occurred to me then that he suspected I had stolen them. My heart gave a jump. Suppose he refused to buy them. Suppose every dealer refused?

'I found them on the outer reef of Rongo,' I said. 'In the Epiphanies. Where I come from.'

He brooded, pulling his fat waxy cheek thoughtfully. I could see he yearned for those ruby harps. All right, I said to myself, better come out with it.

'You think I've nicked them from someone's collection, don't you?'

He was embarrassed. 'There's always the possibility, you know.'

'My passport proves that I was born on Rongo and often go back there. Here it is. Look at it.'

But he was still dubious because of my age.

'Could you bring your father or mother to see me tomorrow?'

'Father's dead and my mother's in the Epiphanies.'

'You must live with some adult or other if you're attending school in Sydney,' he said, exasperated.

'How would any adult know for sure I'd found these shells myself? *You* don't, you say.'

While this was going on a young man was wandering around the shop, looking into the shell cases and taking notes. Suddenly he uttered a yelp.

'You're not saying that pair are actually ruby harps? Pardon me, sir, am I allowed?' He had a distinctive accent.

He didn't wait for permission before reverently lifting

8

one of my shells and turning it around under the light. It looked glorious.

'Do you know I've seen only one other specimen? Are these for sale? Where were they found? Is it in order for me to make an offer?'

The thought crossed both my mind and the shopkeeper's at the same time. If he didn't buy, this man would. Like a hawk the shopkeeper scooped the shell from the velvet, held out his hand for the other, and said: 'I'll just finish my business with this young lady, sir, and then I'll be with you.'

If I'd had any brains I would have asked the young man what he'd pay, but I was too inexperienced. One moment I was hustled into the office; the next, it seemed, I was out on the street with a lot of money. However, I did well out of my treasures, and I knew I might not have sold them at all if the Canadian or whatever he was hadn't come into the shop.

I had a busy morning in the city. People are very difficult with those they regard as children. They ask questions they would not dream of asking anyone over sixteen. However, I did what I had to do, and went on to school.

There was a row about my lateness but I let that pass over my head. With Joanne I was a mouse, but at St Saviour's I was a self-possessed stirrer. I had found that if I allowed my hard black stare to settle on the bridge of any botherer's nose, be she teacher, tennis coach, or boring peer, sooner or later that botherer ran out of steam and stumped off. The truth was none of them knew what to make of me — I was too smart, too much of a loner, I hated sports, I had no boy friend and wanted none.

I didn't know what to make of myself either, though naturally I would never have let anyone know that, not even my sister Sif. Sometimes I felt eleven or twelve years old, full of dreams and romance about life. Marvellous, fanciful happenings. That kind of thing. But I always pulled myself up sternly. I knew I had to look after Sif.

When I returned home I found that Sif had had a cheerless afternoon with Joanne. Joanne was banging things around in the kitchen, Travis was whimpering, and Sif sat with all her corners tucked in, as though she feared that if she moved a finger she'd break something. I looked at her. It was truly no wonder Joanne called her sulky, and I felt a stir of sympathy for Joanne.

'Well,' I said, 'I have your tickets. You're booked on the early plane on Thursday.'

I thought she was going to keel over, so I followed through immediately. 'Rongo,' I said. 'Mother. Dockie. The reef, flowers, coconut palms, the lagoon. Home, Sif!'

She argued no more. But she did say: 'There's no need for you to follow me, Riko.'

'Yes, there is,' I said. 'Joanne gets up my nose, too. I need a holiday with our own kind of people. You needn't worry I'll get behind with school. I can run rings around that dumb lot at St Saviour's.'

'Big head,' said Sif, smiling. She knew I wanted to see her settled on Rongo, to see her safe.

That night I brooded a little enviously over the wad of air tickets. In those days getting to Rongo was adventurous — first the big jet to Fiji, then a small jet to Tonga, then a little workhorse of a plane to our Big Island. After that you had to catch a fishing craft or passing motorboat out to Rongo. But eventually Sif would be in Dockie's house, being fussed over by his mountainous brown wife, Mummy Ti.

On Thursday, before even Giselle was awake and chirping, Sif crept out of the house, took the train to Sydney and a bus to the air terminal and by breakfast time was on the flight to Fiji. It would have amused me to trot sedately off to school and leave Joanne to find Sif's empty bed and have a barking fit. But my sister had said I was not to do that. Joanne could not help being the way she was.

'Sarah seems to have gone, Jo,' I said hesitantly.

'Gone where?'

'Back to the Island. She left a note, Jo.'

There was a marvellous row — ingratitude, madness, where did she get the money, deceitful creature, wash my hands of her, wait till James hears, stop your yelling, Giselle, or I'll put you in your room and shut the door.

Now, for myself, I'd have contacted the police at Nandi airport in Fiji and arranged for Sif to be held there until she could be brought back. She was, after all, under age. But either Joanne didn't think of it or else she did and made no move because she was relieved to be rid of Sif.

'She isn't clever enough to organise this without letting something slip,' Joanne said sharply. 'Didn't you guess anything?'

I shook my head and snivelled into my handkerchief. Pleased to miss another tedious day at St Saviour's, I sat around looking heartbroken. When James returned in the evening, however, I noticed that he gave me an occasional thoughtful look. I resolved not to be too smart with James.

It was he who asked me if I thought Sif would be all right on Rongo.

'Oh, yes,' I replied, 'Dockie will look after her like his own daughter, and Mother will often see her.'

'Your mother,' he said hesitantly. 'I've never been sure — that is to say, Jo has told me, of course, that she is an Island woman and still living, but — well, I gather that your father was on his own during his last years?'

'She went back to her own people,' I murmured. 'She didn't really belong to Rongo, and she was very homesick.'

'She came from another island in the group, then?'

'Something like that,' I said. I wiped my eyes and blew my nose.

'I'm sorry, Erika pet,' he said. 'Didn't mean to pry.'

I felt ashamed. He was a civilised person. I was sorry I had deceived him, and intended to deceive him further.

All this time Travis sat quietly on the floor, white chin in white hand, looking at a book. He was a stick-like child of whom I took very little notice. When he wasn't screeching with terror or rage, he was silent and pre-occupied. I think he was one of the many children who would prefer to be invisible. After James went away to comfort Joanne, Travis gave me a sideways glance.

'I saw Sarah sneaking out this morning,' he said. 'I saw you say goodbye, too. You told a story to Mummy when you said you didn't know she was going.'

For a moment I had no word to say. Then I mumbled something about a person having to tell lies sometimes.

I expected him to prance away to his mother to tell on me, but instead he put his book away and said, 'Yes, I know.'

I remembered he was always being whacked for telling untruths. Now his pinched face flushed. 'Will Sarah stay with my grandmother?'

'Sometimes,' I said warily.

'Mummy won't talk about her. Is she upset because Granny is a brown lady?'

'Maybe.'

The little boy was pale again. He chewed his knuckles anxiously. It was not a nice sight, and I looked away. Then he came to stand beside me.

'Look,' he said.

Dumbfounded I examined the scars on his fingers.

'Mummy had them operated on when I was a baby. Before you came.'

'Did anyone tell you what they were like before the operation?'

'Daddy. But it was accidental. And Mummy was very angry.'

Putting my arm around him, I hugged him. His warm breath fluttered on my cheek.

James looked in the door and smiled approvingly. He thought I was being unusually loving to my little nephew. But I was just recognising.

Chapter 2

It was steaming hot in the airport at Tonga. Yet I shivered with excitement, for within moments the Epiphany aircraft would be loading. I could see it on the tarmac, surrounded by Tongans whose majestic stature made it seem all the tinier and flimsier. They were man-handling on board the usual mishmash of cargo — a calf in a net, red mailbags, drums of fuel oil, crates of beer, frozen hamburgers and all the other junk food the Epiphany people love. Our baggage was already in the freight compartment.

Just as a friendly Polynesian voice called us to board, a late passenger hurried towards the departure bay. I could not believe my eyes. It was the customer from the shell shop in Sydney.

He knew me at once, asking: 'Did you happen to see them load on a scuba outfit?'

I nodded. By this time we were moving through the gate to show our passes. He fell in beside me as though we were old travelling companions.

'I'm Henry Jacka,' he said. 'It's because of you I'm here.'

On the aircraft I tried to sit beside a vast Island lady who brimmed over her seat into the next, but the cabin attendant moved me on, whispering: 'You'll be more comfortable forward, Erika. It *is* Erika, isn't it? We carried Sif about a month ago. What are you doing here in term time?'

I was sulky when Mr Jacka plumped down beside me, fastened his seat belt and beamed at me. I wanted the flight to Big Island to myself for dreaming and planning and watching the islands skid past far below, green dabs of jungle and coconut palms, afloat in a magic sea. I wanted to think about Sif, and seeing her soon. I fancied that my seatmate had bought my ruby harps and heard about the Epiphanies from the shell dealer, but that gave him no right to disturb my peace. I realised I would have to cease being a mild-mannered junior, and sharpen up my hard black gaze.

'Been collecting specimens in Tonga,' he began. 'Here's my card.'

I read his name, which had a little tail of letters after it. Below was the address of an American museum that specialised, I knew, in marine collections. I was impressed but did not show it.

'And I already know you're Erika Magnus.'

That shopkeeper has a big mouth, I fumed silently. I kept my head down and mumbled answers to his questions, while low-lying Tonga glided away in our wake, and only the hyacinth Pacific, dreamlike in a gauze of heat and vastness, was beneath us, endless and mine.

Mr Jacka had a freckled, rather solemn face, and handsome sandy hair. He wore spectacles. He was large, and looked supple in that special way of people who do much diving. He must have been smart to be a field researcher for that museum.

He had, of course, bought my harp shells and was crazy to find some more. Like many experts, he had scarcely heard of the Epiphany Group and was thrilled to be on his way there.

'Heaven knows how many other rarities I might find,'

he said. I could see he dreamed of fame — his own name on a shell.

In the usual adult way he began at once to ask me questions about myself, did I have any brothers, what was my favourite sport, and such garbage. Grown-up persons cherish two great myths: firstly that kids want to be friendly with them, and secondly that all the conversation they desire is chitchat about themselves. Can't they remember how secretive all children are? And as for being friendly, what person of thirteen or fourteen really wants to pal up with an oldie? They are the Them in the anxious game of Them and Us. This oldie, this shell collector, actually said: 'You can call me Henry if you wish.'

What for? I longed to yell. I don't want to call you anything. I just want you to push off. But he wasn't a bad specimen of his kind, so I said nicely: 'Oh, no, I couldn't, Mr Jacka!'

He went on asking personal questions. I went on mumbling put-offs.

'Chatty little thing, aren't you,' he teased after my tenth mumble. I said I was sleepy, having flown straight through from Sydney.

He was apologetic, tucked a pillow under my head, and brought out a textbook. I gazed out into the never-ceasing blue, half hypnotised. I relived the weeks leading up to my departure — the long wait for Dockie's fifty dollars, Sif's blissful letter, sneaking out at dawn that morning (days ago, it seemed) to find Travis shivering, hidden in the hedge.

'I won't tell,' he said. 'I just wanted to ask you something.'

I hugged him while Mr Califano, who had insisted he deliver me at the airport, impatiently fidgeted in his vegetable truck.

'Tell my granny about me,' whispered Travis.

'I promise. I'll be back in a few weeks, and we'll have some conversations. I'm not staying away for good like Sarah, you know. I've left a note for your Mum on my bed.'

The moment I said it I knew I had forgotten to leave that note. It was still in my pocket. One of those double-layered thoughts whizzed through my mind. The top bit let me know that if I gave it to Travis Joanne might punish him for not calling her or his father to stop me leaving. The bottom layer was just a gleeful feeling. Let her worry, it said. Serves her right. Damn Joanne.

In the plane it came to me now and then that I'd been unfair, but I chased that idea away. There was no need to fret, anyway. Jo would certainly squeeze the facts out of poor Travis one way or another. Deciding to think later about Travis, I fell asleep.

I was awakened by a stiff neck, as well as Henry Jacka leaning across me to the window, shouting 'Oh! Oh!' and not knowing he uttered a sound.

The hostess smiled. I suppose she never rode a plane into Big Island without the passengers setting up a yell of 'Oh! Oh!' The residents went on like that because they were so glad to be home, and the strangers because they had never yet seen anything so beautiful. I gazed past my seatmate's freckled ear and there it was, Big Island, clouds sitting on its vermilion crags, streams unravelling over black basalt precipices. All around, like feathery green chickens, clustered the coconut islets, and on their fringe, a little apart, rose the secret castle of Rongo.

Soon I was in the small flowery shed behind the airstrip, and there was Sif, eyes sparkling in a brown face, and

17

Mummy Ti, the size of a house, crowned with yellow hibiscus, and yelling with happiness. I forgot everything then. In a little while we were in Dockie's store boat, bumping across the lagoon to the break in the reef. Mummy Ti tipped up the shaft of the outboard, a wave lifted us and we slid over into the open sea. The night odours of the outer islands came to me, for the swift tropic dark was already gliding over the water, and the flowers that loved mist and moonlight were in a hurry to open.

Dockie and Mummy Ti lived in my father's house, the bungalow behind the store. It had a tin roof with pearly-eyed geckoes for inhabitants, and shutters that were closed only against cyclones. Floors were polished satin black by generations of leathery feet. Everywhere were shells, plants, paintings, carvings, books.

Dockie was a small man like rusty iron with a thin nose I loved. When I was young I thought it was made of play putty, for some accident had given it a little inquiring quirk towards the left. He still had the nimble hands of a doctor.

'Thanks for sending the fifty dollars towards my ticket, Dockie,' I said. 'I couldn't have done it without you.'

'Don't involve me, you wicked brat,' he said. His eyes twinkled. 'Running away in term time! I just hope Jo and James understand, that's all. Fed up, were you?'

'Well, in my note I said I was homesick,' I explained carefully. It was at this point that I really became deceitful. It would never enter my dear friend's head that I would let him think I had left a note if I hadn't. He put his arm around me and said comfortably:

'Oh, she'll understand. Though you might cop it when you go back. Don't let's fuss about it!' He gave me a squeeze. 'You've really come to be sure that Sif is all right, eh?'

'Oh, well,' I said sulkily. I could never pull the wool over his eyes.

Sif had gone to tell Mother I had arrived safely.

Dockie said, 'Matira has your big brother with her, too.'

I was delighted. After Sif, Stig was my favourite person. Mummy Ti called from the kitchen: 'You run off, darlen. Supper can wait.'

As I ran down the crushed shell path to the lagoon I wondered how I could bear to leave the Island again. But I knew I must. I had to finish college, go to University, do very well at University. I wanted to be a marine biologist. It was the dream of my life.

The sea was streaked and sequinned, pale green and full of lights like a great city. Sif was swimming in the warm shallows. When I called, she waved to me. She too was covered in phosphorescence for a moment, then the moon came up and the lagoon went dark. Far out near the reef something like a vast fish leaped and crashed in a smother of foam.

'Wow! that was a big one,' commented a friendly voice behind me.

I gaped at Mr Jacka, petrified.

'I'm really camped on Big Island,' he explained cheerfully. 'Managed to get lodgings with the airstrip manager. But I was keen to see the island of the ruby harp shells, so I came over in a fishing canoe.'

'Stig! Stig!' I shouted. At the same time Sif stood up in the water, waving a warning. But it was too late. My brother Stig ploughed through the lagoon like a half-submerged submarine. He was surprised but not disturbed that Sif and I had a stranger with us. He whacked

19

the water and the sea spouted, moonlight shining through it and showing his tangled fair beard. He hauled himself out on the sand and began to pick at his thigh.

'Damned sea lice, they itch like hell,' he growled in his voice of a bull seal. Sif threw her arms around him and embraced him. Over her head he sent a glance like twin blue daggers at Mr Jacka, who looked like a man half-swallowed in an earthquake.

'It can't be,' Mr Jacka muttered. 'I must have heat-stroke. Travel fatigue. My brain's given way.'

'Who's this jabberer?' boomed Stig.

I stammered out an explanation. 'From U.S.A., plane, shell collector.'

'You!' said Stig. 'What is your President going to do about nuclear experiments in the Pacific?'

Sif and I looked at each other in consternation. It was worse for me because I knew he was a scientist and far from being an ordinary tourist.

'I suppose you don't believe in mermen, young man,' said Stig testily. Mr Jacka slowly shook his head. Stig slammed down his tail in the shallows and wet us all to the skin.

'And I don't believe in astronauts!' he bellowed. *'Prove them to me!'*

Just then our mother rose like a brown wraith out of the lagoon. Though she was old, she was not old like a landwoman. Her hair was a metre long, cloudy in the water like dark weed. On her head was an ornament of blue staghorn coral. I forgot about the stranger on our beach and splashed towards her.

Always when her arms were around me I forgot that Matira had run off to live with her own people when I was four, leaving me to my father and Dockie to bring up. There was enough seaperson in me to understand her homesickness.

'My Riko,' she murmured.

Rikoriko is my real name. It means dancing sparkle on creek water. Too, it sounds to me like the chuckle of a swift creek. But Joanne changed it.

'Hey, you!' Stig shouted. 'What is your nation going to do about heavy metal pollution? Poison wastes dumped in the sea? The air full of muck that would choke a walrus? Why are you landcrabs destroying our world? Have we no rights? Ah,' he said disgustedly, 'there he goes, scuttling away, like all crabs. Just when the conversation was getting interesting.'

'Oh, Stig,' I groaned. 'What shall I say if he asks me about you?'

Stig snorted and dived. He churned away across the lagoon.

'You worry too much,' said my mother. 'The Islanders will treat him as they treat all strangers who come on us by chance. He will go away hoping to forget the whole thing. You'll see.'

'That knucklehead Stig,' I fumed.

My mother gave me a slap, only half playful, for Stig was an important man under the sea and deserved respect. Then she hugged me again.

I thought how different Travis would be, if he were Matira's child rather than Joanne's. He was like a starved plant, too feeble to open. I told my mother about Travis, how he'd been born with webbed fingers and that he had big black eyes like her and myself. She was overjoyed. Joanne was a disappointment to her, the only one without a touch of seaperson, a girl who hated the ocean and got seasick into the bargain. She was a disgrace to the family.

21

Sif and I made arrangements to visit the undersea city next day and returned home. Dockie and Mummy Ti made light of Mr Jacka's unexpected sighting of my family, even though I told them who he was.

'Pooh,' said Mummy Ti, 'a man who collects shells, what is that? He can be fooled, like any other man.'

She twinkled a glance at Dockie.

'If he works for the Friedlander Museum he's no fool!' I warned.

But Dockie laughed. He was confident that our stranger would react in the usual way. He said easily:

'In the first place, Riko, he doesn't know Stig and Matira are your family. And in the second place you know very well that everyone, even the missionary, will give him the standard treatment. He'll think he's had a hallucination because of some rare tropical virus.'

Mummy Ti said triumphantly: 'And you forgetting the earthquakes, old man!'

They beamed cunningly at each other. 'Poor lad!' said Dockie, grinning.

Earth tremors were a way of life in the Epiphanies. No one minded except tourists, and sometimes they minded in dramatic ways, picking themselves up after a little shake had rolled them out of bed, and haring down to the jetty in their pyjamas, screeching for a boat. It was entertaining for us Islanders to see the poor things looking glazy-eyed at the coffee shooting out of their cups, or bottles dancing along a shelf. For us earth tremors were just a part of Rongo, like avocadoes or sunshine.

Very likely, in centuries gone past, if a quake brought down too many green coconuts, or the tide went out and didn't come back for three days, the Rong'ans might have tossed a slave or two into the volcano. But not since the missionaries came.

22

Like all Island kids, I found earthquakes thrilling. It made a person realise she wasn't someone important, living on a big dead ball of rock and silt, but just a frail nothing like a flea, occupying very little space on the hide of a marvellous live monster which every now and then twitched that hide, or trembled in a dream. Earthquakes made me feel *religious*. But tourists didn't feel religious. They just wanted out of there, quick.

I let Dockie and the others persuade me. Adults are supposed to be wiser than children. Still, for a moment or two I was a little sorry for Henry Jacka. He was friendly, and appreciated shells.

We sat down to supper. That night we ate a pineapple stuffed with crisp pork and macadamia nuts, clam fritters and sweet potato pudding. We also had a fruit salad which Mummy Ti called 'a muddle'. It was composed of seven equatorial fruits and some peppery flower petals to give it zing. I went to bed full to the earholes.

'I'm so glad you're here, Riko,' said Sif from the other bed. 'I hope poor old Jo wasn't too upset.'

'I wrote her a very nice note,' I said. 'Better than she deserved.'

I didn't think twice about misleading Sif as well as Dockie. I thought I would get away with it and no one would ever know.

'I'm so happy,' said Sif contentedly. 'Everything's wonderful.'

'Well,' I pointed out. 'There is Mr Jacka. I mean, things could get awkward.'

'We'll hope they don't.' She laughed. 'Didn't he look thunderstruck! He couldn't handle the situation at all — Stig, and Mother's tail. That's why he walked away.'

'I hope he's walking still,' I said.

Sif laughed. 'Go to sleep,' she said.

23

I noticed she still coughed now and then.

It must be hard for cold country people to understand how daylight comes to a tropical island, like the slash of a sword. I lay drowsily looking at stars, and the next moment it was dawn, birds whistling, coconut fronds clattering in the daybreak wind, me jumping out of bed, wild to have a swim. Sif had already gone. The lagoon was as clear as glass. No sign of my sister. She was already out beyond the reef, deep diving with Mother and Stig. So many reef creatures that open their shells, or prowl all night, are not yet home in their chinks and crannies before the sun rises, and so are available to be looked at or played with.

But others get up at the crack of dawn, ready for breakfast. I met a puffer fish who was not glad to meet me. He puffed up until he looked like a scrap of green lace on top of a huge pale wobbly egg. He was quite helpless, drifting slowly about, his Cupid face horrified.

In water four or five metres deep, I half-emptied my lungs and sank down to sit on the bottom. Sif could do this with ease, though she too was only half seaperson. I have to hold on to a rock, and even then my backside often wafts off the sand and stands me on my head. But still, it is almost my favourite occupation. Then the water is invisible, and only the quicksilver, shifting surface of the sea above lets you know you are in another element. Through my eyelashes I watched spider shellfish humping their horned pink shells at a fast crawl over the sand, sometimes turning large, human-looking eyes on me and deciding I was just jetsam that had fallen through from the skyworld. Like many other molluscs, spiders know about the skyworld because they often

24

crawl about on exposed reefs between tides. Then to my horror, I saw a pair of muscular human legs explode through the silver ceiling of the lagoon. The next moment a head broke through as well, and Henry Jacka's salt-blinded eyes spotted me on the bottom.

A bubble of air blupped out of my mouth and dodged up towards him. His head and shoulders came down towards me, I was grabbed painfully by the hair and hauled to the surface. The sunlight hit my eyes like a photoflash.

'You halfwit, you dumb interfering person!'

'Keep calm!' he commanded.

His arm under my chin was like an iron bar. I thought of chewing it, then realised the best thing was to go limp. The moment the crazy man turned me on my front I kicked him in the knees and swam to the beach. He followed.

'Mr Jacka,' I said with dignity. 'I was merely sitting on the lagoon bottom enjoying the scenery and minding my own business. What are you doing here so early in the morning? You are supposed to be on Big Island.'

While he apologised and laughed, I felt my hair to see if it were still attached. Also I sneaked glances out to sea, fearing that Sif might bring Mother or Stig through the reef. My companion explained that the previous evening he had found somewhere to camp on Rongo — an empty fisherman's hut near the jetty. Later that day, he added, he planned to return to Big Island to fetch his baggage and diving gear.

'You won't be as comfortable in that shack as you'd be with the airport manager,' I muttered.

'Ah,' he said. 'But it's on the Rongo reef that I want to dive.'

'We have earthquakes, too!' I blurted.

25

He looked interested. 'Good. Earth tremors really give me a high.'

I was dismayed, knowing what a complication to our family life his presence might be. A column of spray fountained beyond the reef entrance. I knew Stig had sounded. My companion squinted through the sun-dazzle. The next moment there came Sif, streaking across the lagoon. A wake of foam, her wet face smiling, and all at once there she was, her eyelashes stuck in points. She had a flax kit on her back. As she dumped it on the sand a variety of silky tentacles, blushing with anger, sneaked through the holes.

'Will you take the octopuses to Mummy Ti, Riko?' she asked.

The young man's face was full of admiration. No wonder. Sif was beautiful, standing there wringing out her long hair.

'Aren't you the young lady who was here yesterday evening when — when —' his tongue refused to say the rest.

'When I was swimming with my friends, yes,' she answered, composed as you like. I introduced them properly.

'I'm usually called Henry,' said the young man.

'Henry,' said Sif gently.

I sharply slapped a tentacle curling around my leg and departed. I was uneasy. I had a puzzling feeling of almost physical danger. Also I didn't care for the way Sif had spoken to him, open and smiling. Most times Sif was away like a bird. Also, she was not a ready smiler. Then I chided myself. Sif held our ancestry dear. I knew she would not be careless enough to let this pest Jacka guess our secret.

Dockie was drinking schnapps.

'Best breakfast in the world for an old rooster,' he assured me. Mummy Ti didn't like his drinking in the kitchen. She thought he might breathe on the cooker and go up in a mushroom-shaped cloud. So when he had a fancy for getting drunk he went into the store, sitting in the swivel chair that was a leftover from surgery days.

I sat beside him, eating pineapple out of one hand and mango out of the other, and looking around the store, which I loved, because Father always seemed to be there. The building had been slapped together by a Kowloon merchant long before. It was only a great tin roof that resounded like steady thunder in the rainy season; there were no walls at all except the apricot bougainvillea climbing around the roof posts. In the rainy season the floor flooded, but Mummy Ti just swept out the water. In at the back, out at the front, all dry in ten minutes. The store stocked food, liquor, hurricane lamps, hardware, boat necessities, bolts of blazing cotton for the women, and of course aspirin, for like all healthy island people, the Rong'ans ate aspirin like candy.

Sif drifted in.

'What happened to Mr Jacka? You've been such a time!'

'Oh, we were just talking,' she said. 'That pineapple looks good, Riko.'

'I just hope things are going to be all right, that's all,' I said testily to Dockie after she had gone. 'Nuisance of a man! Hanging about and spoiling everything. And now Sif being friendly instead of freezing him solid.'

'Shah, shah, little chicken,' said Dockie benevolently. 'You fuss too much.'

But I worried. Stig, our magnificent brother, saw no reason why landpeople should not learn about seapeople. But Stig, aside from his being a blabbermouth,

27

was as artless as he was honest. He was innocent about white skinned landmen because he had known none besides Dockie and two or three missionaries and our father. He judged all men by the Polynesians. But the Islanders were different. They had always known about the sea tribes. They fished, feasted, and intermarried with them. In their sensible view land birds had no quarrel with sea birds.

Sif and I had often explained to Stig that as far as most landpersons went, our sort was only legend. And legend was a good safe place to be. I pointed out the aggressiveness and curiosity of the white skinned races, their disregard of any species not necessary to themselves. I told him of the few seapeople who had been captured in the past, how they had been murdered and mummified and exhibited in travelling shows, or even worse, kept alive in tanks, to swim round and round until they drowned. Sif said, aghast: 'Don't, Riko, please don't!'

Stig said all he wanted was a man to man confrontation with those who were poisoning the ocean.

'You're drivelling,' I once heard Dockie say to him severely. 'They'd just regard you as bigger and better fish, and wipe you all out in twenty years. Do you want to end in a can, my boy?'

I spent a happy morning goofing off; it was not till late afternoon that Sif and I were to visit the undersea city.

Sif had directed Henry Jacka to the back reef, the best reef for unbroken shells, and he was out there diving now. I hoped he'd find plenty and keep away from the lagoon. However, about two o'clock he entered the store, crimson with sunburn. He thirstily drank a bottle of Coke, though it was warmish, the refrigerator being temperamental. Dockie was asleep in his chair. I had attended to the few customers.

'By the way, Erika,' said Mr Jacka in a confident voice, 'who was the man with the blond beard, the one I saw on the beach last night?'

'Oh, that was just Stig,' I replied. Dockie opened one bloodshot eye.

'I'd certainly like a chat with him,' said Henry.

'He may well be away to meet the whales by now,' said Dockie drowsily.

'You can't mean that he's a whaler!'

'No, he's on the side of the whales,' replied wicked Dockie. But the young man's sandy face was determined.

'You are Dr Copeland, I believe?'

'Correct.'

Mr Jacka introduced himself and continued:

'Possibly Erika has mentioned that last night I witnessed an incredible thing. And two incredible beings. In short, a man and woman with — with tails.'

He blurted out the last word. You could see how he hated saying it. Dockie put his fingers together and looked kind.

'Do you refer to a merman and merwoman?'

Mr Jacka turned redder with relief. 'Thank heaven! At last I've met a person not bent on giving me a runaround. Every one I have spoken with today, even the Reverend Mr Spry — I was beginning to think, well —' he shook his head.

'Goodness,' I chirped, mild-mannered junior once more.

'I take it, Doctor, that you believe in these — these creatures?'

Dockie gazed at him solemnly. 'I would as soon deny the existence of seapeople as I would that of menehune.'

'What?'

'Menehune,' I explained. 'Fairies, some people call them. Great workers with earth and stone.'

'They built the breakwater on Big Island,' added Dockie, 'and our jetty. Many years ago, of course. They live underground, up in the hills.'

Mr Jacka turned redder, but said politely: 'You're joking, of course.'

I was shocked. 'I just hope a menehune doesn't hear you, that's all. They can be very spiteful.'

At that point Mr Spry the missionary came into the store to pick up his tobacco. He knew things like Greek and Hebrew, but he was no hand with a boat or even a fish hook. However, the Rong'ans loved him as they did their souls.

Mr Jacka said breezily: 'Our friends here are putting me on in great style. They say you've a breed of fairies living here called menehune.'

'Oh, no, not fairies,' corrected Mr Spry courteously, 'but a dwarf race, oh, yes, indeed. They come up to about here,' he said, marking off a place on his leg. 'I fancy they were the first settlers in the Pacific. My theory is that they're from South America, for their skins are a coppery brown.'

The shell collector uttered an exclamation and marched out. The missionary shrugged. 'What a very impetuous young man!' he murmured mildly.

Dockie grinned and closed his eyes. I fetched Mr Spry his tobacco and closed the store for the afternoon's rest. Before I did I peeked out to see the young American's rag hat bobbing around near the fisherman's shack he had taken over. I hoped he was angry enough to return to Big Island and the airport manager's civilised cottage. When I ducked under the counter I was sorry to see that

30

Mr Spry had forgotten to take the sweets he always bought for the menehune who had built his church.

Just before sunset Sif and I went to the lagoon. It was low tide, so we clambered around the outer reef, waiting for Stig. The great clams, ruffled with kingfisher blue and green, were open to the sunlight; a nudibranch, an animal flower, purple and rose, performed its mysterious dance in the deepest pool. The sea itself ran like crystal, all on a slant. I thought how long the seapeople live, five or six times longer than we of the skyworld, and how I must die years before my mother, just because my father had been from the land. But I had loved my father; I did not begrudge being half human. To the ocean I was no more important than the small mindless creature inside a blue australwink. But still I belonged to it, though not so much as my sister.

In spite of our father, Sif was almost entirely a seaperson. She had the slow heartbeat and circulatory differences that the sea otters and dolphins have, so she could swim underwater for long distances. But I was not fitted by nature to do what Sif could do, so I often used a rebreather, a small light breathing apparatus. It operates on the closed circuit principle and the seapeople use it for arduous dives or long journeys. For they, like all mammals, are limited in the time they can exist without refilling their lungs.

'Hey! You girls stuck to the reef like limpets?'

There was Stig, grinning, his hair and beard washing around in the water like yellow seaweed.

Sif took a flying leap into the sea, and she and my brother were away like arrows. I dived in and swam after them. But in a flicker of time the dolphins were there beside me — common dolphins, small and sinuous, their large black-ringed eyes sparkling with joy at seeing me again. I was never quite able to tell them where I disappeared to during my absences from Rongo. They knew about cities, having often watched them puffing and grumbling away on the shores of harbours. But school they could not understand.

Dolphins are such scamps. They shoved their noses under me and turned me head over heels, fled down into the depths after me and bore me back to the surface on their backs, bursting with me into the sunlight in a glittering explosion of water. There I bobbed, breathless, while they flirted and romped. Looking back towards the land, I saw a figure on the exposed reef, and the flash of the westering sun on binoculars.

'Quiet!' I thought warningly, and my friends sank down, only eyes and snouts above water, their powerful tails turned inward to keep them upright.

'There's a man on the reef watching us!'

They set up a whistling chorus. 'We'll go and play with him!'

'No, scatterbrains, we have to follow Sif and Stig. Come.'

Away we flew underwater, passing like a flock of birds along the outer rampart of the reef. I looked amongst the dolphins for my special friend Emily. Emere we called her, Island style.

'Where's Emere, you water monkeys?' I thought.

'Emere sad.'

As dolphins, unless they have a bellyache or something equally unimportant, are never anything but cheerful, I paid little attention. Before long the city wavered into sight. My heart filled with delight as it swelled wraithlike through the invisible flower-blue water. Long shafts of sunlight pierced the sea, for the city was not set deep. Indeed, if it had been, the dolphins could not have accompanied me, for they are surface creatures and must live close to air. They nudged me excitedly, and were silent. They fluttered and trembled. One rested his warm undersnout on my shoulder, and softly chirped. Did he say a word? Is dolphin speech in words after all? They use so much telepathy, even the seapeople cannot say how many of their communications come in through the ears or through the brain. But I thought the dolphin uttered a word, not 'queen' or 'goddess' but something like that. Maybe 'angel'.

For they are angels, the whales, holy creatures that during their long majestic lives, do nothing except what their Creator planned for them. Their world is the Garden of Eden, unless man enters it.

From below us there rose something like a floating island. As it drew upwards, this vast dappled being, the dolphins and I wafted away like leaves, for it created its own watery winds.

She was a humpback whale, almost fourteen metres long. Her slender elegant muzzle passed me. The under-jaw, which can balloon into a pelican pouch when the whale is feeding, was tightly pleated, the mouth primmed shut. I feathered away, gliding my hand along the skin which is like the skin of an apple, but softer. One white flipper, long and supple as a wing, deftly lifted itself so that I should not be hurt. A plum-blue shining gaze took me in and let me go, as the whale moved onwards without pause or deviation.

'She comes to bear her child,' said the dolphins, 'she is happy.'

'I know,' I thought back at them. 'But hurry now, Stig waits for us.'

Our city was rebuilt only a hundred years ago with the aid of the Rong'ans. It had been wrecked when the volcano Krakatoa blew up, causing massive shifts in the sea floor from the Celebes to the Tonga Trench. There were many other cities, of course, in every ocean warm enough to sustain life. Our founding city, the Shelter built when our ancestors realised the Pacific continents were submerging year by year, is now at the bottom of a mile-deep rift. We were told this by the lord sperm whales, who hunt in such places. There it stands in the black, changeless undersea. Though for generations none has viewed it, that lost city is our sacred place.

Of course, all over the planet humans have done the same thing when extinction threatened — gone under the loving sea. It is true that for some reason dwarf beings such as piskies, trolls and menehune, prefer to vanish underground. Still, the same instinct is at work, and this is why there are legends of elves and mermaids everywhere.

Sif and Stig impatiently swam around beside the city gate. It was not really a gate, but a type of lock, as in a spaceship. The dolphins kissed me and darted away upwards, to feed and play.

Chapter 3

Now I have to tell you what I later learned from Mr Jacka and other people. After his conversation with Dockie and Mr Spry, Mr Jacka was as mad as a hornet. He felt that the two old men were making a fool of him, and he could not understand why. What had he done? Were they against shell collectors? Americans? Museums? Coming from a hospitable nation himself he could not understand why they wanted to tease him. Even the blond-bearded man at the lagoon had abused him as if he were an enemy, called him names.

'Landcrab!' brooded Henry. 'Why landcrab?'

Again and again he went over the scene at the lagoon. Had the moonlight tricked a travel-weary brain into imagining he had seen a man and woman with tails? He could not believe that. But he could not believe the tails either.

The menehune had been the last straw. He tramped up and down inside his hut, fuming about fairies until the mosquitoes drove him outside. He noticed Sif and me leave the bungalow.

He was so annoyed with us all that he followed us to the lagoon and watched from the beach. When we disappeared from the outer reef he scrambled over the coral as fast as he could to see where we had gone. But all he saw was a schoolgirl romping with a herd of dolphins. Then I, too, sank down into the sunset dazzle, and vanished.

When I did not come up again he kicked off his shoes and dived in. He swam around shouting for me and Sif. This was brave because he feared that maybe sharks had got us. The sun had almost set, the sky darkened with seabirds fleeing towards the land. In a few moments it would be night. Distraught, he hauled himself out and ran for the shore. His one idea was to get help.

Running on live coral is like running on knives. Dockie said that when Mr Jacka fell up the verandah steps his feet and lower legs were as bloodied as if barracouta had been worrying them. He gasped that the Magnus girls had drowned; Dockie had to get help immediately; he himself would take out a boat and search.

Mummy Ti uttered a horrified yowl and waddled off for warm water and bandages. Dockie hoisted the young man up the steps, saying firmly:

'The girls are all right. You hear me, young fella? They're champion swimmers, safe as sprats in the water. For Pete's sake, what made you run over coral in your bare feet? Surely a man of your trade knows better than that.'

'He frightened for Sif, old man,' said Mummy Ti, returning. She subsided at Mr Jacka's feet like a deflating balloon and began to bathe his cuts and scratches. They were already inflamed.

'Never mind that,' yelled Henry distractedly, 'what about the girls?'

'Simmer down, lad. They swam down the coast a little way, and climbed out without your noticing. I know them better than you do. They'll be home for supper as they promised.'

Probably the unworried calm of Dockie and Mummy Ti was what cooled off Henry. He felt he had been made to look a fool once again, and this time he had managed it himself. He became aware of his tortured legs and feet.

'I'd better have an antibiotic,' he said to Dockie.

'Got none here. You'll have to go over to Big Island see the M.O. Want me to get out the boat and take you?'

The young man was resentful and obstinate. He didn't want to be under an obligation to Dockie or anyone of our family. He shook his head.

'Have some common sense,' urged Dockie. 'Coral poisoning could lay you up for a week.'

'No doubt the menehune will come and look after me,' said the young man bitterly.

Dockie could be very commanding when he liked.

'You've had a shock,' he said. 'You'll change those wet clothes and have a brandy. And a bite of supper if you feel like it.'

Grumpily Henry agreed.

'Besides,' added Dockie 'I want you to see the girls when they come home. They'd wish to thank you for your concern.'

What with the fright he'd had, his throbbing feet and legs, and his feeling that the white Rong'ans had treated him outrageously, Henry was in a fightable mood. Added to that, he remembered he had lost his boots and binoculars to the rising tide.

He came straight out with it and demanded of Dockie why everyone he met seemed determined to pull his leg. He had to shout some of this, because Mummy Ti had turned on Radio Fiji and had settled down comfortably to listen to a talk in Hindustani on Girl Guides. She knew no Hindustani but she didn't mind what the noise was, as long as it was noise.

Dockie was in a quandary. He put Henry off this way and that, saying: 'It's an Island tradition. Well, you

37

know Polynesians, always on for a laugh. Put it down to our isolation, we've a weird sense of humour.'

He sought to break up the discussion by shouting at Mummy Ti to turn off the quack-box. Mummy Ti was tired both of the Girl Guides and the argument.

'Maybe you tell him the truth,' she suggested in Rong'an.

Dockie could not believe his ears. 'Are you mad, Fat Woman?'

'I think this one is clever,' she said. 'And to be trusted, too. Look at that face. You foolish old dog's bone, he is young and so is our Sif. He would never do anything to injure her or her people.'

'Tell him the truth?' bawled Dockie, horrified, hearing nothing else. He and Mummy Ti went at it like fighting foxes. Mr Jacka sat there, hurting, waiting for us to come home.

When we landed on the lagoon beach Sif was chilled and a little breathless. She put on the cotton shift she had thrown amongst the dry rocks, but still she shivered.

'It's living in Sydney for so long,' she excused herself. 'I'm as out of condition as a jellyfish.'

I scarcely heard. I was half in a dream, for the under-sea city still glimmered in my head. There is a poem somewhere that speaks of such a city.

Ceilings of amber and pavements of pearl, it says, and I often wonder how that poet knew.

The moment Henry heard our sandals crunching on the shell path he lurched out to the verandah. By now his cuts were stiffening up and he was in real pain.

'Where have you two been?' he demanded. 'Where did you get to? Are you all right?'

Of course we did not know what he was yelling about.

'Dear God,' he said, and I heard a sort of croak in his voice as he looked at my sister, 'I thought you'd drowned.' I heard his voice, I saw the expression on his face and it was as if a spear went through me. No words came to my mind. Everything about me, my blood-stream, my brain cells, spoke out in some Stone Age way: 'This man will take Sif away from me.' There he stood, his hair sticking up, his shortsighted eyes blinking, his bare legs bandaged — and I could have killed him, he was so dangerous.

I shouted: 'You were spying on us!'

Dockie must have seen the red in my eye, for he ordered:

'Run off, Riko, and have your shower. Quick march now!'

I screamed at him like a parrakeet. I could have killed him too.

'I'm not a baby, I will not go and have a shower. I want to know why this man was watching me with binoculars from the reef. Why is he following us around? Snooping!'

'Of course Mr Jacka was not spying,' said Dockie sharply. 'You forget yourself, Erika.'

'Well, maybe I was snooping in a kind of way,' admitted Henry. 'Though I believed I was just looking. I'd be surprised to find anyone who wouldn't watch a young girl playing in deep water with a flock of dolphins.'

'Dolphins?' I jeered. 'What are you talking about? You're off the wall.'

No use. Mummy Ti, already upset over the argument with Dockie, began to blubber. Dockie put on a thunderous face and spat out in Rong'an: 'You ought to be more careful. What's the matter with you, lass?'

39

'That's right, blame me!' I spat back.

'Look, we can sort this out,' began Mr Jacka.

'Oh, shut up,' I cried. 'Why don't you just buzz off? You're not wanted on Rongo.'

'Don't mind,' said Sif in her gentle way to Mr Jacka. 'Riko is just tired and cold.' She put her arm around me, but I pulled away, glaring. Mummy Ti gave me a slap, and I slapped back.

'You be ashamed, you Riko!' she said, and getting me by the scruff and the rear of my swimmers she trundled me down the passage to the bathroom. Being hustled by Mummy Ti was like being propelled by a cyclone. I came slapbang up against the tank of tropical fish that formed the west wall of the bathroom. The key turned in the bathroom door.

'You get under the shower and scrub away that bad temper, you Riko! You make shame for me!'

'I'll put all your fish down the loo!' I shouted back.

I'd read about people being rocked by a sudden realisation, and now I knew it was true. I was shaking as if I had a fever. To lose my sister! I had simply never thought of Sif getting married and going away to lead a life without me in it. We had always been together. We always would be. Some day I would be a qualified marine biologist, but I had always counted on Sif's being there, helping, encouraging, talking things over. *Being there.* Now I saw that was a child's way of looking at things. I was fourteen, but going on six years old as far as Sif was concerned. It was such a shock I felt I was going to throw up. But although I coughed and retched over the toilet bowl, nothing came up.

Feeling half crazy I put my head against the cool glass of the fish tank. A tiny polished fish like a sliver of silverfoil drifted past my nose and was eaten by an anemone. I was glad. An infant octopus lifted itself by the middle like a rag on a stick and flowed away behind a rock. I knew a small cod often sheltered there and I hoped the octopus would get golloped too. Down by the jetty the outboard motor hawked and caught. Without thinking twice about it I knew Sif was taking Henry Jacka over to Big Island and the hospital.

My mother had abandoned me, my father had died, I had withstood Joanne's coldness and impatience, and I had not cried. But now I did. A true black hate arose in my heart for Henry Jacka. I knew how the dolphins felt when they ganged up on a shark that was sniffing around their young, and nearly hammered him to death with their snouts.

'I can't lose Sif!' All of me, heart and brain, muscles, everything, silently shouted this. It was like a person shouting 'I must have air!' For me Sif was like air. Everyone else in my life had gone, even Dockie and Mummy Ti, for they were not with me most of the time. But glad or sad, Sif had been with me. I could not imagine life without her.

Mummy Ti came in and made me take a boiling shower. She yearned to cuddle and comfort me; I could see it written all over her face. But I ignored her, stalked past her, got into bed and pulled the sheet over my head.

'You a ratty little handful, Riko,' she said in a disappointed way, 'and I afraid you always be a ratty little handful.'

I lay awake hating everyone, even Sif, who probably had gone off in that thin cotton wrapper. She would catch a chill and get sick, and then I would not be able to go back to Sydney. I had the chill turn into pneumonia, a long illness. I would have to stay and nurse her, I would fail my final examinations, I would end up never

41

going to University and it would be all her fault, or rather Henry Jacka's fault. Tears of sympathy for myself splattered on the pillow. I knew Sif would not return to Rongo that night. It was usual for lategoers to sleep overnight at the hospital. I pictured her that moment, talking to Henry Jacka, the boring busybody, being sorry for his stupid feet, when anyone with half a spoonful of brain knew you never ran shoeless on live coral.

When the dawn wind arose, I awoke in an empty room. I could hear the banana plants clapping their hands in gardens all over the island. When I went to the lagoon, shoals of sprats were already fizzing through the pearly water. Gannets, their wings furled about their legs, lanced downwards after them. The world was pure, innocent, rapturous, yet disgusting feelings enveloped me like a bath of acid. My dolphin friend Emere came as close as she dared into the shallows and splashed her flippers to make me notice. Her glistening head protruded from the water like a seal's.

'Emere want you,' she whistled.

'I'm busy. I've things to think about,' I thought sullenly.

'Emere need Riko.'

Into the horrible confusion of my fear, jealousy and hate came the pure voice of her sorrow, like a stroke on a bell.

'Go away, go away,' I said furiously. 'I've troubles enough of my own.'

Her head sank without a ripple.

Henry Jacka's interest in my sister was plain to me. It was true she was only seventeen, but Henry, if indeed he was that, was no more than twenty-four. I was used to people falling in love very early; it is the Island way. Somehow I had to get Mr Jacka to leave Rongo before

Sif fell in love with him. What I needed was someone to help me make his life so miserable he would be glad to catch the first boat out. And who would make a better ally than a menehune?

I ran back to the house. Mummy Ti had breakfast on the table. She was beaming, eager to forgive me.

'I don't want any breakfast,' I said, jamming my feet into tough old sneakers.

'Where you going?'

'Mind your own business,' I said. She aimed a slap at me. I dodged, and ran. I could easily have told her I was going to visit the menehune. She knew I had friends amongst them. But I did not. I was too angry.

That anger drove me at a run up the first steep hill paths. I had to sit down on a boulder to get my breath back. Suddenly I felt mean. Not only because of Mummy Ti, but because I had turned away Emere. I wondered why she had been so sad, and for a moment my heart was sad too.

'I can't think of that now,' I told myself, and set my face towards the high country behind the settlement.

As I climbed through the leafy glens, past the Steaming Cliff, where boiling water tumbled down a hundred metres into an eroded mud valley, I felt through my soles the fine shake and quiver of the island. Rongo is like a needle stuck upright in the seabed. All the Epiphanies are tall islands. They rise from the ocean floor like pillars or palm trees, not spreading at all at the base. The Hawaiian group are tall islands too; if you measure them from root to crown they are the tallest mountains on earth.

Not so many centuries ago, menehune also lived on Hawaii. They did much building — sea-walls, fishponds and ceremonial platforms — for the ancient Polynesian

43

tribes. But when Hawaii became more populated and there were wars and noisy confusions, the menehune packed up and sailed away to Tahiti. I never did learn whence our menehune tribe had emigrated. When I asked old Bluebush, who was boss man in my childhood, all he would say was: 'We came down the star path.'

Now Rongo was becoming overcrowded for our menehune. They had retreated further and further into the foothills of the old volcano. That meant hard going for me, across causeways of wrinkled prehistoric lava. I had to scramble on all fours up formations like black glaciers, hot as iron to the touch, bearing only rich green cushions of creeping thorn. When I came at last into the crow's-nest menehune country, I realised at once that I was being watched from the stunted scrub or the fallen grey boulders that looked like pigmy elephants.

In a gully canopied with vines, a little old broad thing emerged from behind a rock. It had a bare chest, stiff grey hair, and a kilt of plaited flax. On a cord around its short strong neck hung the lid of a coffee tin, brightly polished.

'I see you still have the gift I gave you when I was young, Father Axe,' I said politely.

Hands hard as bone, with broken black nails, took mine. We rubbed noses in the family manner, Axe and I, for he had known me since my father carried me up the mountain in a backpack. We sat in the shade and conversed. Courteously turning his eyes away from my shirtfront, he congratulated me on becoming a woman. The menehune thought a great deal about women, because they had so few. Thus there was no increase in population. All over the Pacific their numbers were dwindling. My father once told me this is nature's way of dealing with a totally non-progressive species.

Menehune are certainly non-progressive. They believe that the skills developed thousands of years ago are sufficient for any kind of era, including this. Mr Spry called them Stone Age people. However, from what I learned from Bluebush, and a blind, gabby old creature like a twisted tree root who seemed to be Bluebush's grandfather, they long, long predate the Stone Age. The gabby person spoke of the time of ice, when only underground dwellers survived. And before that, he said, there was the time of fire. That sounds like some fearful earth catastrophe, a planetary collision, perhaps.

Like most subterranean people, the menehune are deathly afraid of fire and do not use it at all. When I was small I sneaked fifty metres or so down one of their burrows. As this was forbidden, my father spanked me in front of the assembled menehune. I was greatly shamed. Still, I remembered the burrow. It stank like a lion's den. I also saw that the little men used earthlight, that mysterious greenish light often observed in elf mounds and barrows, but not understood by anyone who lives on the surface.

Menehune have plain strong object names like Manu, Ika, Poa. These mean Bird, Fish, Mouth. Other names translate as Rock, Trout, Pig.

Fifty years before, a boy was captured by a zealous missionary and baptised Paul. This was quickly changed into Poro, which means Backside, and is a historic joke amongst the menehune.

Mr Spry did not try to convert them. Still, he told them Gospel stories, which they enjoyed greatly. He once told me their version of the tale of the Three Wise Men.

Listen! There was a poor woman with no burrow. She bore her manchild in a cave where mumu (cows) *sheltered. The One Who Made All said: 'That is a good woman and a fine manchild'. He put a star with hair (a comet) into the sky and frightened three big chiefs. Whoo, they wet themselves with fright. Running to that cave they gave all their riches, stone axes, hoes and diggers, flax garments, to the woman. So all was well. Then the star with hair went away, and the rich chiefs took all their presents back.*

Mr Spry was unable to convince his listeners that such was not the true end of the story. He was kind to them, but unfortunately he introduced them to sweets and chewing gum.

While Axe and I were speaking, from the corner of my eye I saw Pig behind a tree, wiggling and wheedling and showing his woeful brown teeth. He was crazy about sweets. After a while, since Axe had agreed with me that Mr Jacka should be chased away one way or another, Pig was called from his hiding place. He was as old as myself, but twice as wide, with a head of orange spikes. Axe was humiliated by the spikes.

'He will not leave his hair alone. He dips it in the hot spring,' he fretted.

'It's *my* hair!' cried Pig defiantly.

Axe rolled up his eyes. I could see the pair had this conversation regularly.

'All those minerals will make your hair fall out,' I cautioned.

'Don't care. When I'm bald I'll paint my skull like a bird's egg.'

Axe's bellow made no impression on him.

Pig wore jeans, which he had stolen from a clothes line down in the village. The legs were far too narrow for his muscular limbs, so he had slit them up the seams. The jeans now flapped about his legs like the cowboy chaps you see in ancient Western photographs. Pig was unbearably arrogant about his jeans. He was convinced they were magic and could turn him into a modern boy. He was that rare creature, a menehune who wished to join the rest of the world. So he caused great anxiety to his tribe.

Thrilled with the idea of terrorising Mr Jacka, Pig jumped high in the air and jigged like a monkey with a bee sting.

'Me and Mud will tie him up in a sack and drown him in the mangrove swamp.'

'No, you won't. You'll do just as I say.'

Pig pouted out his lips. Menehune are immensely strong. Even left to himself, Pig could have overcome Mr Jacka.

'You hear? I just want him scared away from Rongo, that's all.'

Scowling, Pig nodded. He knew I did not like his friend Mud, a shifty little brute with a squashed nose.

We worked out a hassle campaign for Mr Jacka. It was not the first Pig and I had planned, but of course I had been younger then.

'Spooky noises around his shack at night?'

'Dead fish under bunk.'

'All his papers hidden.'

'Small turtle among blankets and sheets?'

'Good thinking, Pig. And sea urchins in his boots, that very prickly kind.'

Pig thought it was a good idea to shin up a coconut palm with Mr Jacka's best jacket, and hang it from the highest point.

'Always drives tourists yelling crazy,' he chortled.

47

The first move in the anti-Jacka war was to be a phony burglary — everything in his hut overturned and thrown around, the captions taken from his photographs if possible, his passport and travellers' cheques put in a different place from where he had left them. I arranged a signal that would bring Pig down to the village when the time was right. For his reward he demanded a large bag of caramels, and my little pocket radio. Axe was against the latter. He felt there must be something unhealthy about a box that contained so many people.

Axe did not object at all to our unkind plans for Mr Jacka. He listened, grinning. There is in menehune this hard mischievous streak, quite wicked sometimes. Occasionally I had known them to take a dislike to a workman, or even a tourist, and make his life complete hell. But if they like you, they can't do enough for you.

I left them arguing about the radio. I knew Pig would win. Any fourteen-year-old is a champion pesterer, but a fourteen-year-old menehune is the best of the lot.

Oh, I was happy running home! I had solved the problem. Menehune are marvellously good at scaring people. When I was younger, Pig and I had often worked as a team to frighten off tourists we didn't care for. We certainly gave them something to write about in their MY TRIP books. Very soon Mr Jacka would fly away and leave Sif and me in peace. I bounded down those fearsome lava glaciers like a goat. Now and then a gloss of water showed through the trees. Rongo was rich in streams, dewponds, springs. There was hardly a valley that did not have its little lake, full of clouds.

Soon I could see the lagoon, and on it a canoe like a peapod. I loved the lagoon and the canoe and the whole island so much I burst out into blissful singing.

Around the corner on the homeward track I met Sif, coming to look for me. She put on a stern face, but she was not good at it.

'You know perfectly well, Riko, the rule is we tell someone at the house where we're going.'

'I know, I know,' I said. 'I'll remember next time, okay?' and went on singing. Sif joined in. From a taro swamp an Islander raised a muddy arm to wave, and his deep voice joined our song.

Then the dogs began to yelp, some close, some far, for Polynesian dogs are musical, too. Sif and I stopped singing and laughed. I noticed she was smiling and laughing a lot more than was her habit. If that was because she was happy to be back home, I was glad; if it was because of Henry Jacka, I wasn't.

'What happened about him?' I asked. 'You know, Mr Jacka.'

I hoped he'd been left in the hospital, preferably strapped to his bed of pain. But Sif had brought him back that morning to the shack by the Rongo jetty. He was to rest for a few days, with Mummy Ti to feed him and look after his damaged legs. I stopped feeling blissful.

'We weren't very kind to him,' said Sif. 'Dockie feels we owe him something, and so do I.'

She told me about Henry's plunging into what he thought were sharky waters to look for us. A sweeping tide of panic rose in me. I wanted to burst out with pleas and warnings. But the crafty person inside me was well practised. I kept quiet and put a soothing expression on my face while Sif went on:

'He must be awfully clever, don't you think? But he's a very modest person. He said he isn't anyone important at the Museum, just a junior. He's on his own time at the moment, too. He was due for a vacation, and he thought he'd take it on Rongo.'

'Oh, great,' I thought bitterly. But my voice, when it came out, was the one I used to Joanne to placate and deceive.

'Oh, well,' I said meekly, 'a rest here may be just what he needs.'

'He's really interesting,' said Sif. 'Fun,' she said, after a while. These words upset me more than if Sif had raved about him. She was not in love with him yet, but she had already seen he was a person she could love.

'Riko,' she said. 'Please apologise to Henry for what you said last night.'

'I'll tell Mummy Ti I'm sorry I went on the way I did,' I said sulkily. 'But why should I apologise to him? Serve him right. He butted in, and no one asked him to.'

'He meant well,' she said. 'He really did, Riko. I don't want him to think you're bad-mannered. I want him to know you as we do, as a really great kid.'

'I'm not a kid,' I ground out. 'I'm fourteen with a skyhigh I.Q. and what's more, old Axe the menehune thinks I'm a woman.'

Sif laughed. 'Well, whatever you are, please make friends with Henry. Even if it's only because I'd like you to.'

'I might,' I grunted ungraciously, and ran on ahead, hoping she'd understand from the way I banged down my feet that the whole idea gave me the sicks.

I told Mummy Ti I was sorry for behaving like a hellion, and was forgiven. But it was not till the next morning that I could swallow my resentment enough to visit Mr Jacka. He was propped up on his camp bed, his swollen, awful-looking legs on a cushion, and he was busily writing away in a yellow spiral-bound notebook.

'Hi, Erika,' he said. 'Come to keep the leper company?' He gestured at his legs.

'I've had coral poisoning,' I said gruffly. 'I know it hurts. What I've come for is to apologise for saying all those gross things the other night.'

He laid his notebook and pen aside, and took off his glasses. Without them his eyes looked humorous and kind.

'But you aren't really sorry, are you, Erika?'

'No,' I blurted. 'Sif asked me to apologise, and so I have. But you *were* spying on me, Mr Jacka.'

At that point I heard a low grumble like that of a distant aircraft. And through the window I saw the grass on the hillsides bow down like a green wave before oncoming air pressure.

'There's going to be an earthquake!' I said, delighted.

'Oh?' he said. His hand darted out and moved his pen away from his notes, and just as well, because the next moment it squirted ink halfway across the room. The shack shook, things fell off the wall, and the chair I sat on skidded for the door. It was all over in a few seconds. I don't know what I hoped, but it wasn't what I saw: Mr Jacka putting his glasses back on and looking calm and benevolent.

'And now to get back to spying, Erika, I was not doing that at all. As I told Dr Copeland, I was just watching you and the dolphins. And don't waste your time turning that death ray look on me.'

I realised then that I was giving him the frowning black glare with which I subdued teachers and kids at school.

'I've a young brother who does the same thing,' he continued pleasantly. 'You might as well know, teenagers

51

are not sacred cows to me. Just something to put up with until they turn into humans.' He picked up his notebook. 'See you around, Riko.'

'Only my family are allowed to call me that,' I snapped.

'Oh, nonsense!' he said and gave me a grin I could have liked him for, if I hadn't hated him. I stamped off in a fury of disappointment. He really did like earthquakes. He even knew about pens spurting ink. I was as mad as a hornet, and yet somehow I was pleased to know that there was at least one other person, not an Islander, who wasn't scared during a tremor.

During my Rong'an holidays, it had always been my joy to pack a little food and goof off somewhere for the day. But for the next few days I fooled around the plantation and the lagoon, keeping an eye on Mr Jacka's hut. I thought Sif and Mummy Ti visited it far too often. On the third day Dockie had one of the big Island boys carry his planter's chair — it was made of wicker, with a long leg rest — into the shade of a wild fig tree. Dockie and the Islander helped Henry, hopping and stumbling, into the open air. All day he sat there, writing away in that yellow notebook. Now and then he glanced at the store, or the ocean, and I believed I knew what he was thinking.

'We're going to end up in a piece for *Scientific American*!' I thought, horrified. Up till then I had worried about Mr Jacka only on and off. Now I settled down to being anxious nearly all the time. For it was easy to imagine the flood of the world's media to tiny lost Rongo; tourist planes landing in droves on Big Island; the *National Geographic* mounting an expedition; flocks of scuba buffs bubbling off to explore our undersea city. And the menehune getting the huff, which they

52

would, and sailing away to live somewhere else. I felt certain that all this could happen, and my heart filled with doom.

But could I tell all this to Dockie? I could not. He was still stiff with me because I had behaved rudely to Mummy Ti, whom he loved dearly. His was a Scots anger, freezing and unforgiving.

'But I told Mummy Ti I was sorry, and I *am* sorry, Dockie!'

'Humph!'

He twitched his nose sideways as though to say 'That doesn't alter things!' Then he said:

'And that young fellow. From another country at that! Buzz off, you said, and called him a snooper, not to mention your disrespectful belief that he was off his head.'

'I apologised to him, too, and you know perfectly well I did,' I cried, my temper tickling. 'Anyway, he's a danger to the seapeople, you can't deny that. He's a scientist.'

'I'm no fool, you know,' said Dockie severely. 'I don't need a pushy wee bundle of cheek to work things out for me. You take too much on yourself, Erika. Let the grown people handle this. And keep your mouth buttoned.'

I went off seething. I'd never thought of Dockie as an adult but of course he was one, boring pretentious creatures that they were. Besides, his calling me Erika hurt me dreadfully.

But if Dockie usually knew what was going on in my head, I also knew what was in his. He had been upset by Stig's outburst, and worried by what Mr Jacka had seen at the lagoon. Perhaps he was most anxious about Sif's friendship with the young man. Still, I thought it wisest to shut up for the present. How *were* the oldies going to handle it, I wondered? I could have bet they did not have an idea in their heads for gently shooing Henry Jacka away to some other island in the Pacific, preferably one near the South Pole. No, it was safer to rely upon Pig's monkey tricks and my own brains.

All this time Emere had tried to coax me into the water. Now, as I sat on the sand, sulking, plotting, she lay on her side in the shallows with one eye in the air. That eye was so big, round, and soft, all at once I felt again the love that had been driven out of my heart by fear and jealousy.

'What is it, Emere?'

'Emere has child. Come and see.'

I waded into the water. Dolphins' children stay close beside them for a long time. They are like shadows, swimming above or beside, their movements exactly synchronised with those of the mother. But Emere, when she nuzzled alongside me, was alone.

'Where's the child then?'

'Come.'

With one light hand on her dorsal fin, I swam beside her. Like whales, dolphins must shelter in calm bays to bear their young. As everyone knows, each mother takes with her a friend to ensure that the baby is helped to the surface to take its first breath.

'See!'

Amongst the rocks floated a small bloated black and white body. The waves whacked it against the rocks. Emere shuddered away as though she could not bear the sight, for dolphins passionately love their young.

The dead baby dolphin had a grossly malformed head. The blowhole, which normally has a hinged flap to form a watertight valve, gaped wide. The infant could not have lived more than a minute or so.

'Oh, poor Emere,' I thought. 'Your child was made wrong.'

'Why?'

The water boiled as Emere's companions surrounded us. They fondled her kindly, and two or three of those with infants pushed their children towards her, inviting her to share. But Emere hung motionless in the water as if dazed. Then she speared away into the indigo distance. Only one old female followed her. I swam to the reef and sat upon a rock. The water was deep, and some of the dolphins were able to rest their snouts on my legs or feet. They all burst into speech together.

'Shah, shah!' I said. It was from the dolphins that Dockie and I took this hush-word. 'One at a time. You first, if you please, old father.'

The great bull of the herd had hung back, silent and majestic. Now he swam forward, and the smaller dolphins ducked under and slid away to give him room. Common dolphins live to the age of eighteen or so. This herdmaster was almost that age. Soon he would be too slow to keep up with the troop. He would be left behind and the sharks would eat him. Or he would do what some weary captive dolphins do; sink down to the bottom and stop breathing. It is my belief that old or sick whales do this also, which is why newly dead whales are so rarely washed ashore.

The bull said that during the last birthing season many dead and deformed children had been born, and even more this current year.

'Why is this?' I asked.

He stood upright in the water. I knew he wished me to touch him. Long ago my father taught me you must never touch a dolphin near the eye, ear or blowhole. I put my hand on his warm brow. Pictures came into my mind. A vast oil slick greasing the ocean with sinister rainbows. A whale trapped in it, a minke as slim as a mullet, exhausted and rolling.

I saw a coral reef, dead as a doornail after a thousand years of gorgeous life, poisoned by herbicides and fertilisers leached from farm soil and sent down rivers into the sea. I saw penguins so sludged with chemical waste that they were no more than blind suffering bundles of congealed tar. And seals and dolphins and whales ill and dying, bearing freakish young, because they are on the end of the food chain and the fish or krill they must eat are polluted with lead, mercury, and other destroyers.

I turned my mind away from the herdmaster's.

'I did not do these things!' I burst out.

'Riko can speak for us to those who do them,' came the chorus.

'I'm too young,' I replied bitterly. 'They don't listen to me any more than they would listen to you.'

They did not sink down and vanish, as I thought they would, for dolphins are the most courteous creatures and never argue. They stayed there, looking at me, making squeaky-gate noises.

'I'm sorry, I'm sorry!' I cried, but I was not so much sorry for my helplessness as for my belonging — half, anyway — to a species of beings that without care or love would poison a whole world. For the earth is a water planet, and the Pacific holds most of that water.

It wasn't until I was halfway to the bungalow that I realised that if the dolphins and seals and whales were on the end of the food chain, so were the seapeople. If the pollution of the oceans continued, soon Matira and Stig and all the others might die. The race would become extinct. I was frightened and dismayed. I had to tell Dockie. This was his business as well as mine. No matter how cross he was with me, he would have to listen to the dolphins' story.

Dockie was in his surgery chair, halfway to being drunk. Dockie drunk was not a person who was silly or abusive or soppy. He just became more Scots — curt and often sarcastic.

'I have to talk to you, Dockie,' I burst out.

'And I have to talk to you.'

Beside his empty whisky glass was an opened letter.

'This morning I went over to Big Island to get the mail,' he said. 'This letter is from your sister Joanne. Perhaps you remember Joanne, Erika?'

'Hell,' I thought, and my heart fluttered. Aloud I said: 'Oh? How are they all? I meant to tell you about Travis. He . . .'

'Stop your prattle. You lied to me, Erika, you lied to all of us. That's one thing. And worse than that is the way you sneaked out without a word to Jo. Cruel and cowardly, that's what it was.'

'I did write a letter,' I protested. 'I just forgot to leave it.'

'You should have told me that when you arrived here. I would have let her know you were all right. She has been very worried and distressed, and no wonder.'

'But I thought Travis would tell . . . '

His eyes were like blue icicles. 'So he did, but only after a whole day. He was frightened. He's but six years old, after all. I'm ashamed of you, Erika.'

'You're mistaken if you think Jo would worry about me and Sif,' I said furiously. 'She's just piling on the

57

drama because she wants to get us into trouble. She was pleased to see the back of Sif, I can tell you!'

'Be that as it may,' said Dockie 'she's had enough of the pair of you.' He picked up the letter and read: "Ungrateful, unco-operative, unloving." Well, you and Sif know best about that. What all this adds up to is that she'll have neither of you back again. So now what are you going to do about college, University and all the rest?'

Everything went out of my mind. I gaped at Dockie.

'That's not fair!'

'I think perhaps it is.'

But already a vision of a free life showed itself. No Joanne picking and scolding, no arguments, no dreary house!

'I don't care. I don't need Joanne. I can go to boarding school. And live in college when I begin University.'

Dockie shook his head. 'There's not enough money. There's not been enough since your father died. We've managed so far only because you and Sif lived with James and Joanne. James provided you with clothes and board and even paid for your holidays back to Rongo. Aye, they've done their best, those two. I give them credit for it.'

His words did not really register with me. They sank into my mind, ready to be looked at later. All I took from them at that time was the fearful knowledge that I was done for. There was not enough money to educate me further. I would never be a marine biologist. I might as well be dead. Sif was content to live out her life on this enchanted island, but I had been made for other things. The whole world called me.

'God!' I groaned.

'And watch your mouth, too, my girl. I blame myself

for this latest escapade of yours,' he went on morosely. 'Slipping away to visit your home — I thought of it as a bit of adventure, something I might have done myself when young. I thought Jo would have guessed at it and let you go, knowing you'd be as safe as the Bank. I must have been daft. She's mortally offended, and I've no doubt James feels let down as well, poor lad.'

'I'll drown myself,' I croaked.

'No, you won't,' said Dockie. 'It's time to open the store. You'd better get used to looking after it, for I expect that will be your job from now on.'

A long time after that dreadful minute, it came to me that all I had to say then was that I had done it all to help Sif, who had been always half unwell and as miserable as a wet cat. Dockie would have listened, because he knew how much I loved my sister. And he would have believed me, too, because when I arrived on the Island he had understood at once that I had come mostly to see that Sif was happy.

If I had explained he would have given me credit for the way I had plotted and planned, and maybe understood it was necessary to deceive Joanne, because I believed her to be that kind of person. I might have ended up in Mummy Ti's immense kind arms, which was just where I needed to be.

But instead I put on a haughty face and drew myself up. I wasn't quite sure what that meant, but I had a shot at it.

'Open the store yourself,' I said hotly. 'And you needn't think I'm beaten. I *will* go to University, and I *will* be a famous scientist. You just see, Dockie.'

I left the store. But I was hardly outside before I went to pieces. How would I do those things? It became important to find Sif, who didn't know what had happened, and who would speak up for me when she did. I needed her. I wanted her.

But when I finally saw her amidst the sun-dazzle on the lagoon, dawdling around, looking at the coral and the fish through a glass-bottomed box as she loved to do, she was not alone. Henry Jacka was with her. I have excellent sight, and I could see they were chatting away, pointing things out to each other as if they had been friends for years. It was like a knife in my heart.

Like all young people I had a secret hiding place. Away up the valley behind the bungalow ran a track, so over-grown it could not have been found by an adult. A person had to get down on all fours to travel along this green tunnel, which perhaps had first been made by wild pigs in the long ago. There was a snug smell of grass roots, brambly vines and marshy water that I could neither hear nor see. This track led to a little round clearing. It too was hidden from the outside world, but once it had been a garden. I had found there wild dwarfish descendants of old Polynesian vegetables, the kind that had never been grown since the white man came to the Pacific — edible ferns; knobbly violet-skinned sweet potatoes; the pre-historic yam, so fibrous it wore people's teeth flat.

At one end, stuck askew in the soft earth, was a god no taller than myself. Carved from soft volcanic tufa, he was old and worn and snubbed-off everywhere, but not as much as he would have been if he had spent his centuries out in the rain and salty wind. He was Tane, tree-person, forest guardian, and in the old belief, a god who had had a great deal to do with the creation of women, and consequently me. He was dear to the menehune, and indeed some had visited him recently.

Wilted flowers, a string of vivid blue berries, and a bunch of parrot feathers lay around his toes. I sat down amongst this holy debris, leaned my head against his navel, over which his three-fingered hands were clasped, and tried to work things out.

Chapter 4

The missionary before Mr Spry, so I had been told, said it was an abomination that modern people should give respect — if not actually get down on their marrowbones and pray — to the old oceanic gods. He tried to lever some of them out of the ground with a crowbar. But then the tree fell on him. Mr Spry, however, said sensibly that the gods had been around the Pacific for thousands of years and it was nothing more than good manners to treat elderly persons nicely.

This Tane was not beautiful. He had his tongue out further than was polite, and his eye sockets, lacking the rounds of pearlshell that had once been there, were mysterious and watchful. But he had the comfortable feeling of a tree, or a sunwarm rock, or even a reliable dog.

When I was young and occasionally invited a whacking, I used to go to my secret hiding place and ask Tane to wreak vengeance on Mummy Ti — thunderbolts, tidal waves, or an upset stomach. But he never did. Even when I was in Sydney, so far away, he was always in the back of my mind, full of peace and wisdom so old there was no following it.

That god said nothing at all to me while I steamed and sobbed my way through fury, shame at being found out and grief at my lost chances for fame in this world. By the time the western sun was shooting diamond rays through the treetops, I was left quite empty except for thoughts about Joanne that would not go away. In fact,

I was too exhausted to think of anything else.

To be told that she and James had paid so much for our upkeep! James could not be rich. The Lindfield house was well-organised, and boringly clean, like the inside of a jet aircraft. But it was not what anyone would call a rich house.

Even when Joanne had been cross with Sif, she had never flung at her cruel true words about being a burden. When I thought of the hateful things I had thought and said about our sister I groaned with shame. But it sounded like a cow mooing, so I stopped.

No wonder Joanne was so often impatient and irritable with us. With the added responsibility of two young sisters, one of whom was wasting her education, she and James probably had a hard time making ends meet.

One of the worst things was that, in my heart, I didn't really want Joanne to be anything but the dreary creep I had always thought her. This made me feel very bad. To feel wicked is one thing, and can be rather thrilling. But to feel contemptible and snakish, that's lowering.

When Pig wandered through the trees, looking rather like one of them, a stump perhaps, I could not even bring myself to say hello.

'You got a toothache?' he asked. 'I hear you making a pain noise.' He knew about toothache because of his ruined teeth, poor Pig. He sat down beside me and with a flourish took a cigarette out of his frizzy orange hair.

'This is for you, Riko.'

I had never tried smoking, because Dockie would have killed me if he'd smelt as much as a whiff about me, but I was so cast down I took the cigarette.

'Where're the matches?'

Pig went almost pale.

'Sorry, Pig. I forgot about fire and all that. Well, this is no good to me, so you'd better have it back.'

He took it, absently chewed it up and swallowed it. It seemed to have no effect, but I was past bothering.

'I've had a bad time, Pig. Awful.'

It was certainly my day for blurting out what troubled me, for all I had told Tane I now repeated to Pig — Dockie's anger with me, my unfairness to Joanne and how I could never really like her even though she was a good person after all. My worries about the dolphins and the seapeople, my fear that Mr Jacka would take Sif away from us.

Pig said no more than the god had but he put his short arm around me. It felt as if it were made of twisted wood. Then he plopped a kiss on my ear.

'Oh, quit it, Pig!' I howled. 'If there's anything I don't need just now it's a sloppy menehune.'

'But we get married when I grow up,' he protested. He was always telling me this. I suppose it was because there was no young girl of his tribe to be a possible wife for him, unlucky Pig.

'I'm not the right shape to live in a burrow,' I reminded him. 'I'll grow big. As big as Sif, maybe even as big as Mummy Ti.'

'I put flowers and these other things before Tane so he make you love me,' he said dolefully. 'I do anything for you, Riko.'

'We're friends, isn't that enough?' I asked. But it wasn't. Just then I heard Mummy Ti calling me. I thought I'd better run; I didn't want any more trouble. Pig would not say goodbye, but remained squatting at the feet of the god.

Dinner was one of those awful meals where everyone is very polite and no one looks anyone else in the eye. By then, I had remembered that I'd gone to tell Dockie about the dolphins and the poor freakish baby. I would have told him then, somehow I would have, even if I'd had to yell. But what was the use? He sat in his big chair like a statue, his eyes shut. He ate nothing, being as drunk as a duke. Mummy Ti whispered that she had told Sif about the letter and the rocketing Dockie had given me. Sif whispered that she had gone to the store at once to explain, but he had only glared and told her to hop it. So there we were, pushing food around our plates, all three miserable for different reasons. Mummy Ti's lip began to tremble.

'Oh, don't, Mummy Ti,' I begged. 'It will all come right in the end.'

No use. At the first tragic grunt Dockie's eyes snapped open.

'Fat Woman!' he snarled 'I will not have you blubbering.'

'Wahhhh!' Away she went to the kitchen, roaring her head off. Dockie rose, and like a robot clunked off into the store. Sif began to clear the table. She comforted Mummy Ti, reminded her that a movie was showing at the schoolhouse that evening, and persuaded her to go. As with all Polynesians, Mummy Ti's tears were brief summer showers. In no time she was tying a purple scarf around her hair, putting on her sneakers, and beaming with pleasure. In the doorway she paused: 'When that old dog's bone fall asleep, darlens, put a blanket over him. He catch cold easy, poor old ruin.'

Like all islands, Rongo was chilly at night. You could hear mysterious movement in the air above — warm waftings from sheltered valleys, scented with vanilla and

65

wild coffee. From the sea the biting wind was so seasoned with salt that sometimes, after a night walk, you felt you wanted to wash your hair. Sif and I sat in front of the kitchen fire, and I explained about the note I hadn't left for Joanne.

'You should have done what we agreed you'd do,' said Sif. She sighed. '*I* can't talk. I haven't written to her yet about leaving Sydney. So if you've been unfair to Jo, so have I. Everything happened in such a hurry, and since I've been back home I just haven't thought of anything but Rongo and the family. I'll write to Joanne,' she said, 'and I'll explain that everything you did was for me, and ask her to forgive us.'

'She won't forgive me,' I muttered. 'And I'll spend the rest of my life right here, weighing out chickenfeed and sugar and feeling my brain turn into rock.'

Sif gave me a squeeze. 'Don't you worry. We'll find some way for you to get to University. When Dockie's sober again he'll see reason. We'll talk it over then. We'll look for more ruby harps. And Henry thinks there may be other rare shells in these waters, really valuable ones, because the Epiphanies have never been fished out. Henry will advise us,' she added eagerly.

'Oh, Henry!' I said fiercely. And in a moment out it came, all my fears for Sif and that young man, my longing to keep her with me for ever all mixed up with dread that somehow he would learn about the seapeople and reveal their existence to the world, in order to earn himself a glorious Ph.D.

Sif sprang away from me. 'He isn't like that at all! Even if he did learn about the sea tribes he wouldn't . . . he wouldn't do that!'

'There, you're defending him already,' I accused. 'Next thing you'll be in love with him.'

66

Sif's face flooded with pink. Even in the firelight I could see it.

'That's dumb, Riko! How could I? I hardly know him. We just talk, that's all. We talk about things I've never spoken about with anyone before.'

'You can talk about them with me!' I cried. The words came out in a furious yelp.

'Like we used to,' I choked.

'But it's different with Henry,' said Sif. 'He's more my age. It's fun to go around with him, to be friends.'

Desperately I argued: 'Well, just suppose, suppose you did fall in love. He'd take you to America away from us — Stig and Mother and Dockie and me. Away from the sea, too. Have you thought of that? And you can't live far from the sea. Remember how you felt in Sydney, Sif. He wouldn't understand.'

Sif jumped up. 'I'm going to have a shower.'

'But, Sif!'

'No,' she said, quite severely for Sif. 'I won't talk about it. You're going on like a dopey kid about things I haven't even thought about.'

But I saw that she had. She whisked out of the kitchen in a huffy way, and five minutes later whisked back again, her clothes off and a towel around her. She said: 'You must get used to the idea that I'm grown up now, Riko. And I want to keep growing up, too!'

'Why?' I wanted to yell after her. Suddenly I hated the idea of growing up for myself, and for my sister too. I longed for her to be seventeen for ever. It could not be, and yet I wanted it.

Sif did not return to the kitchen, so I took a blanket and covered Dockie. I put some wood on the fire, for I felt cold. Cold, lonely and muddled. I almost wished I hadn't followed Sif to the Island. After a long time

I sneaked into our bedroom. Sif had gone straight to bed. She'd fallen asleep with the lamp burning. There were the marks of tears on her face, and that puffy look girls get when they've been crying.

I was so miserable I even thought of going to the school to join the movie crowd, just for company. Far out beyond the reef there was an enormous splash, and then another. The manta rays were playing in the dark, erupting from the deep like vast pale kites. I couldn't see them from the verandah, for it was a very black night. It's wonderful to see them when there's phosphorescence about — they shoot out of the water like starships, dripping greenish fire. But there was no phosphorescence that night. The racket from the schoolhouse was deafening, feet hammering, loud music, laughter. The movie was one of the videos that the Administration sent over from Big Island twice a week. The Rong'ans liked monster movies best, and then comedies and cartoons. Laughing was their favourite thing. They could retell a joke and fall about crowing for weeks after they'd first heard it.

But during a lull in the racket, I heard, much nearer, a succession of unexpected sounds. A scuffle, a muffled cry, grunts, something crashing over, and then gravel rattling under hurried feet. Night fishing was done around Rongo, of course, but not on movie nights. Anyway, these were not night fishing sounds, which are the clunk of a lead sinker into water, the creak of rowlocks, fish frenziedly splashing.

The sound came from the direction of Mr Jacka's hut. A man who is badly lame can bump into things or fall over, and that did not concern me. But the feet on the gravel road? I went to the gate to see if his lamp was shining, and it was not. That gave me another idea;

68

maybe Henry had hobbled off to see the film, in which case I might be able to sneak a peep at his notes. I forgot my troubles, rushed to get my flashlight, and went off to the jetty. The shack's door was open, Henry Jacka was not there, and yet I could see he had been. He had been writing at the table. His pen dribbled ink on an untidy heap of photographs; the lamp chimney was cold. The place was disordered — papers tossed on the floor, a chair overturned, blankets dragged off the bed.

I could smell menehune. All became clear. Pig had not waited for my signal; he had just gone ahead and hijacked Henry. Perhaps that was his idea of doing something for me in my troubles. Pig and Mud, I thought, for Mud smelt riper than Pig by a mile.

I turned the beam on a makeshift bench along one wall. I had seen that bench before. There Mr Jacka had laid out all his new finds, beautiful shells of unusual colour and markings, each with a neat note about it, and the temperature and depth of water where it had been found. But there were no shells now. I ran outside. All the specimens had been thrown out the window and many stamped on. The collector in me was horrified. There is so much work in shell collecting, not only the diving and searching, but the careful removal of the animal within, the cleaning and scrubbing. As Henry collected for a museum, I was sure all his specimens had been perfect. But not now. I really felt bad, not about Henry Jacka, but about those lovely lost shells.

The big yellow notebook lay under the table. I pushed it down the front of my shirt, and raced back to the house to get Sif. No, I thought suddenly. That way the family will learn I made a pact with the menehune to scare Henry off the Island, and Dockie will scorch me to the ground. The memory of my first conversation with

Pig returned: his desire to drown Mr Jacka in the mangrove swamp.

'Heavens,' I thought, 'if those two dingalings have taken him there, he'll be scared all right. The mangroves at night would spook anyone.'

It occurred to me then that maybe Pig had the right idea after all. That creepy place, the black water sucking stealthily at the trees. Crabs over everything like lice, slithering, slithering.

I knew Henry Jacka would not be harmed. Pig would not do anything against my wishes. Somewhat cheered, I poked the yellow notebook deep into the hibiscus hedge and set off for the swamps. They began some distance north of the big lagoon, where several creeks came down into a long arrowhead of estuary. In the silt carried by these mountain creeks, twice daily flooded by salty tides, grew the murky fairy forests of the mangroves. Sif thought they should be called witch woods but I felt witches are too human for mangroves. I remembered that there are evil fairies, full of dark spite and vicious tricks. Such fairies would certainly live amongst mangroves, those strange, unnatural trees. Their leaves are the richest green, a gleaming green. Their fruit, which float away and form little colonies of their own, are crimson. Yet within the groves the light turns back upon itself; the sunshine does not care to steal between the sodden black trunks and intertwined dripping branches. A mangrove swamp is trackless, yet somehow full of tracks — rocket-shaped flurries where a mudskipper fish has travelled from sea to land; three-cornered birdprints; the scribbles of mudworms. Always an almost-silence hangs over the mangroves. The water noises are stealthy — shush, shush, make no noise unless you want to wake something you wouldn't like to meet.

The moon had risen now. I could see the black mass of the mangroves blotting the horizon. I could smell them too, the faint stink of foul gas bubbling from underwater breathing stalks.

Running along the road I thought that perhaps Mr Jacka ought to be left in the mangroves to get the fright of his life. On the other hand I didn't want him to be in bad trouble. Or me, or the menehune, come to that. Although they deserved to be punished for what they had done to the shell specimens. I felt sure that was Mud. Useless destruction would amuse him.

But now my problem was how to find Henry in that maze of holes, deep channels, shifting sand and muddled black trees. All I could do, for a start anyway, was to call his name.

At that point I heard laughter. When the moon rose I had switched off my flashlight, and now I almost fell over Pig and his chum Mud, rolling around cackling their silly heads off. I skewered them in a circle of light and told them what I thought of them. Mud sat there like a toad, grinning. His coppery face was blotched with white from injury or disease, so he really did look like a toad, with stony bold eyes.

Pig pulled a long lip and stuttered: 'I did it for a surprise, Riko. I thought you'd be pleased.'

I knew very well that was what Mud had told him. But Pig should have known better. I thumped him hard on the head. This was a wrong thing to do because menehune regard the head as sacred. Their big insult is: 'I'll eat your head.'

Pig looked stricken, and Mud lolled out a big tongue and rolled away into the scrub. He vanished like magic in the menehune way. Pig wanted to flee, too. I could see his toes twitching.

71

'Talk!' I shouted. 'Or I'll pull your rotten orange hair out.'

After you've had your sacred head thumped, it is menehune etiquette to stalk away, saying no further word to the offender. Then at a later time there's some kind of duel. I was never told what, because that is sacred too. But I think that blood must be shed, maybe a great deal of it.

But now, in his surprise and shame, Pig lost his nerve. He stuttered out excuses. Longing for some devilment, Mud had persuaded my poor friend to visit the village and watch the movie through the schoolhouse windows. At that time, young menehune were forbidden to watch films on the grounds that they would become blind. When the pair spotted Mr Jacka at the back of the schoolroom, they thought it a great chance to carry out the phony break-in Pig and I had planned for Henry. They vandalised the hut, and were busily loosening the valves on the scuba gear when Mr Jacka returned.

'Tried to light the lamp, he did,' said Pit in excuse. He shuddered.

The upshot for Mr Jacka was a gag between the teeth, a sack over his head, and a fast jog between two menehune along the road to the swamp. I groaned. If Dockie ever found out my part in all this my life would not be worth living.

'Where did you put him?'

Those two Stone Age thugs had tied Henry to a tree on one of the patches of solid ground that dotted the swamp. Islands, we called them. I knew this one. Beached on its ocean side was a rotting ship's longboat; we kids had played mutinies and castaways in it when we were young.

72

'You've let me down, Pig,' I said sternly. 'I said no violence. If you or Mud ever say a word about this, you are gone menehune. You assaulted and kidnapped that man. Suppose he complains to the police?'

I knew, and Pig knew that the single cop on Big Island, a football-crazy Islander who could go for three years without arresting anyone, would with his last breath deny the existence of menehune. Still, Pig took fright. He vanished. I had one leg in the cold water when he reappeared. He came back because he knew the cord with which they had tied Henry's wrists might have tightened in the wet. He dumbly held out his great treasure, his knife.

'Thanks, Pig.'

Still he lingered. I could read his honest face. He was wondering if he would still get his reward, the caramels and the radio.

'Do you deserve anything?' I asked. The water was freezing, and the words came out in a bark. Pig shook his head mournfully and flickered into the darkness.

'Mr Jacka!' I shouted. 'It's Erika. I'm coming to help.'

The flashlight seemed dimmed somehow. Its light was soaked up by those thousands of dripping, leprous trees, and the pitchy water sucking at their exposed roots. Those roots glistened and shimmied with crabs. It was hateful, the pits. Why, I asked myself, was I going through this horror scene just to help a person who meant nothing but trouble to me?

With that I fell into the water amongst all those snaky roots. My flashlight did too, but fortunately it was a floater. I grabbed it, threw it up the bank, and seized a branch to help myself. It gave way with a glug, and stinking black water or sap gurgled down on me. It was so disgusting that I leaped out of the water like a mudskipper and landed on my face in the muck. My flashlight, sizzling and steaming in the gloom, was like a star of hope. If it had gone out I think I would have splashed back to dry land and left Henry to his fate.

But I staggered on, falling into pools, blundering into heaps of fallen boughs, starting back from goggle-eyed fish rising in the channels to stare at the light, until at last I saw the skeleton of the longboat. I was gasping with fright and fatigue by then, but I managed to croak out: 'Are you there, Mr Jacka? Mr Jacka?'

'Where the hell do you think I'd be?'

He was more bad-tempered than I could have imagined. He had just managed to work out the gag and his tongue must have felt as if he'd been chewing socks. He started asking me a million questions.

'I don't know, Mr Jacka. I don't know anything. Keep still while I cut you free.'

His wrists were tied around a sturdy tree with fishing line, which is tough stuff. However, I soon hacked it through with Pig's knife. Mr Jacka and I, unfinished mud statues, surveyed each other.

'Do you know the way out of this place?'

'I knew the way in, didn't I?' I was falling down with weariness and this guy asked me stupid questions. My hand trembled as I fumbled Pig's knife into my shirt pocket.

'What's that?' Henry grabbed my wrist, and took the knife from me. It was a flake of black obsidian, sharp as glass, set in a handle of carved ivory. Axe had used it when I first knew him, and before him, very likely, dozens of other menehune had prized this Stone Age tool. Mr Jacka turned the light on it, tried its edge and said, 'Wow!'

'Where did you get this?'

'Found it,' I said vaguely, 'Somewhere. Mr Jacka, please can we go home? I'm whacked.'

In a moment all his anger disappeared. His eyes shone excitedly.

'Archaic Polynesian,' he muttered, 'or then again . . .'

'Give me back my knife!' I demanded peevishly, and reluctantly he returned it. I pointed out the way home. As we sludged along he said: 'How did you know where I was? Did those kids tell you?'

'Uh huh,' I said, cautiously.

'How old would they be? I've never come up against boys so strong. If they hadn't jumped me, maybe I'd have held my own but . . .'

'I think it was just a bit of devilment,' I said. 'They didn't mean any harm. A sort of joke. But they get too rough.'

I remembered the shells then, and thought what a blow it would be to Mr Jacka when he discovered the loss of his specimens.

'Some joke,' muttered Henry. 'You people have the worst sense of humour. Would you mind if I borrowed that stone knife tomorrow, just for a few hours?'

'Oh, I don't know,' I muttered, putting a whine into my voice. 'I might be going fishing, and it's my fishing knife.'

He did not press me.

We splashed over the last channel and heaved ourselves up on the road. The moon was quite high by then; owls were calling. Mr Jacka and I plodded along in silence.

'What's your brother's name?' I asked, just to break it.

'Martin.'

'I like that.'

'He doesn't.'

Just then we saw ahead of us the bobbing fireflies of coconut fibre torches. Mummy Ti and Sif and a crowd of Rong'ans had come to search for us. Sif was very relieved.

'You're nothing but a worry to me! I ought to give you away.'

She turned to Mr Jacka. 'And you're not much better, Henry.' Henry pulled a sorry face. At least I think he did, under all the mud. In a moment everyone was laughing.

When Mummy Ti had returned from the movie, she had woken Sif to ask where I was. Sif had admitted that I'd been very depressed over Joanne's letter, and Mummy Ti immediately had me drowning myself or something equally unlikely. They hurried to ask Mr Jacka to help search, but found him gone and his shack in disorder. After that they roused the neighbours, who liked nothing better than a midnight jaunt and a big hullabaloo.

In fact the whole thing became jollier by the minute. Henry seemed to enjoy it. He waved his hands for silence, and two great clods of muck flew off on the nearest Islanders, who almost died laughing.

'Everything's all right now, folks,' he said. He explained that some of the boys had played a joke on him, but no harm was done, and I had dug him out of the swamps before he caught pneumonia.

The Islanders eyed one another, and two or three sniggered. They knew the menehune had been involved somehow.

'No need to make a fuss,' said Henry, scooping mud from inside his shirt collar. 'A man has to take these things as they come. But I'm going to ask you now to leave me alone. Fun's fun, and you've had plenty of it, but I have to get on with my work.'

That pleased them. Some laughed and clapped, and even whacked him on the shoulder in the way they have.

'You a lovely sport, Henry!' cried Mummy Ti, beaming.

In spite of all, I felt he had taken the whole thing very well. I was quite proud of him. Not proud enough, however, to give him back his yellow notebook.

By the time I got back to the warm kitchen, I realised that the whole affair had shaken me. With a little ferret like Mud involved, things could easily have gone wrong with Henry. He had been sporting about it all, as Mummy Ti had recognised. I stood under the shower scrubbing my hair, and found myself thinking how much I would have liked him if he hadn't liked Sif so much. However, that didn't bear thinking about, so I put on my robe and went back to the kitchen, where my sister and Mummy Ti were making toast and waiting to hear my side of the adventure.

Sif was a little awkward with me at first. But as I told my story she forgot about our earlier set-to. I had decided to tell the whole tale to Mummy Ti and my sister, just in case any of the Island kids were blamed for roughing up Henry Jacka. My own part in the affair I didn't confess entirely; I thought nobody in the family was ready for that. About those damaged shell specimens I felt really bad, and I told Sif so. But she thought he would not take it too badly, as there had been nothing exceptionally rare amongst the collection.

'Now he'll have to stay longer on the Island,' she said happily. 'You and I can help him collect, Riko.'

So much for my great idea for scaring Mr Jacka away from Rongo. Now he'd be with us for weeks and weeks.

Mummy Ti shook her head over the menehune. 'Those little rats,' she said affectionately. 'I'd like to take the flyspray to the lot of them.'

The next day I wrapped my pocket radio in a piece of plastic and took it to Tane's clearing. Sooner or later Pig would find it there. Inside my shirt was the yellow notebook, which early that morning I had rescued from the hedge. I was itching to read it, and yet scared too, for I did not want to learn that Henry had guessed at the existence of the seapeople. At that time I was not at all ashamed about stealing and reading his notes. If anyone read mine now, I'd go right through the roof.

First of all I said my prayers to Tane, not exactly to the little old worn-down statue, but to the feeling that hovered around that green feathery place, a kind of warm but stately personality. I could smell the lemony odour of crushed sweet-grass, and hear an Islander blowing a conch trumpet on some inland hill. He was probably calling his plantation hands to morning tea-O, nothing romantic. But still it sounded romantic. Then I sat down to read the notebook.

The first conclusion I came to was that I was absolutely right in wanting to be a marine biologist. Henry's notes on molluscs, seaweeds, and shore and reef flora were so fascinating I forgot to riffle quickly through the pages until I came to some mention of Matira and Stig or even me and the dolphins. He described several species of our small octopuses, the ones that live in the seagrass gardens. Octopuses are intelligent and charming. Being so fond of them I was quite put out; I felt they all belonged to me. He was interested in sea cucumbers, too. Tearing myself away from these fascinating rock eaters, I flipped over the pages until I read: 'For a time I could not write about this, but during my first evening on Rongo, I saw something hallucinatory in the lagoon, a man and woman with tails.'

Pages and pages followed, of theories, speculations and detailed description of his own doubts. That was how I learned what Henry had thought and felt after his sighting of Mother and Stig. There were lists of comments:

Spoke English.

Man very blond but woman Polynesian type. Very beautiful.

Young Magnus girl familiar with them.

Older sister seemed anxious, shouted some words in Rong'an. (?)

Why was writer addressed as landcrab?

Strong views about conservation. Surely odd that he should bring up this subject within two minutes of our meeting?

Landcrab?

I'm a nut case.

But in the end Mr Jacka had decided that he had been neither hallucinating nor mistaken. The people in the lagoon were real, knew the two Magnus girls, and were aware of what was going on in the world.

It is my belief, he wrote *that they are inhabitants of Rongo, perhaps isolated and backward, living away from the ordinary Islanders and not sharing traditional village or tribal life. Remnants of lesser tribe? Original inhabitants of Island, now very few, and disregarded by others?*

How can I describe my relief! He was so far off the truth he was out of range altogether. Tane's battered

79

knee was near my nose so I gave it a kiss of gratitude. Then I read on:

> But this does not explain the tails. It is true that all sea mammals have tails of a type, and foot or paw bones are to be found within flippers and tails of even so large a creature as the whale.

He went on a good deal about the kind of muscles required to operate a tail, the value of tails to swimming creatures and so on. The notebook concluded: *At this point, it is my theory that the Lagoon People are forced to lead an unpopular and somewhat deprived existence.* Here I laughed aloud, remembering my mother's fabulous jewels, the pearls used to ornament the houses, the undersea city's inexhaustible store of gold ingots, coins, sculptures salvaged from sunken ships. I returned to the notebook and read on: *They may well have the use only of scanty or infertile land, and so get most of their living from the sea. Therefore, to facilitate constant swimming, they have invented a tail. This appendage is really an unknown kind of wetsuit.*

The world fell in on me then. Or so it seemed. I could not believe that this man had guessed. He was wrong about my family living on land, but if he could guess right about the tails, he could guess right about everything else.

You can read every book there is about mermaid sightings, and not one gives you a hint of the simple secret. Perhaps it is too simple.

Tens of thousands of years ago, before our tribe first went undersea, the tail had already been invented for water sports. It was a clumsy thing in those days. As our people have sound technology in all those things that concern their welfare and comfort, they refined the tail until it became the powerful swimming aid of today.

Half the secret is in the length, though few people notice that in drawings of mermaids the tail is far too long for the rest of her body.

Nevertheless, through the centuries Nature has changed the seapeople to suit their environment. Like whales they can store oxygen and thus breathe infrequently. Many, like Travis, are born with webs between their fingers. They have the circulatory differences that Sif and Stig luckily inherited, and can resist cold and water pressure. Stig could dive to great depths. He said that he changed shape, as whales do. He felt his face become long and inhuman. He saw things magnified. These things are not fantasy; scientists have learned how they happen from their study of whales. You will notice from folk legends that mermaids have usually been seen at dawn and after sunset. The reason is that their eyes can no longer bear full sunshine. Of course, some can. My brother Stig, for instance, had the same brilliant sight that I have. Another little difference amongst the seapeople is that some children, not all, are born with small, feeble feet, so that they have difficulty walking. My mother, Matira, was one of these. In the sea she was a queen, but on land she was half-crippled, limping and always in pain. This was half of the reason why she returned to the sea, the other being my father's love of the bottle.

Sif and Henry Jacka were diving from a small boat on one of the bays. Mr Jacka's coral poisoning was much improved, and he thought the salt water might finish the cure. So I could not tell Sif what I had found out. And I couldn't speak to Dockie either; he was as sick as a poisoned pig after his spree. Anyway, I didn't really wish to speak to him. I felt that this problem was one for the seapeople. I longed to see Stig, and pass over the problem to him. Perhaps, I mused sorrowfully, I really was too young, never quite sure of the right thing to do. But I would tell Stig about Emere's baby as well.

Mummy Ti was sitting under the poinciana shelling peas. Its green bower put lacy shadows on her face. She looked at me wistfully, and I realised I had not been very nice to live with since I returned from Sydney.

'I *have* been ratty,' I said repentantly. 'I don't know what's the matter with me, Mummy Ti.'

'You growen up, darlen,' she said. Over my dead body, I thought. But of course I didn't say anything. I gave her a hug and a kiss.

'Where you goen, love?'

'Just swimming.'

I grabbed a towel off the wire netting that covered the herb garden to stop the cats from scratching in it, picked up my goggles and snorkel, waved her goodbye and set off.

It was queer though. I looked back at Mummy Ti, brimming over in the doorway of the bungalow I loved, and for a moment the thought came to me that one day she too would go on her way, like my father and Fredrik, that brother of ours who came between Stig and Joanne, who had been trapped while exploring a wreck, and so drowned.

I could live without Mummy Ti more easily than I could live without Sif, but I did not want to.

Chapter 5

My sadness pleased me; it seemed a mature way to feel. I could see the whole scene on film — sunny clouds towering over the Island, the skyblue lagoon, and this courageous girl swimming across it.

I swam for the gut where the ocean rushed through. Though not wide enough for a boat, it was a good passage for swimmer or dolphin. Rather exciting, however; you had to wait around treading water until a big wave receded, then whoosh out into the open sea, amidst an avalanche of white foam. Of course, you had to make certain the coral didn't rip you like an old rag, but I was experienced.

Coming up half-drowned, I stretched out my arms to welcome the dolphins. But all around drowsed the supple sea with no dark head breaking the surface. I could not imagine why. Disappointed, I ducked underwater and set off for the submarine city, swimming slowly and strongly.

There was a law in our land family that no one ever swam alone outside the lagoon. The sea family followed this rule as well. My brother Fredrik, who died before I was born, was exploring by himself when he was pinned down by a falling beam in that Spanish wreck. Very soon I glided above it, and wished my brother well. The outer reef was littered with wreckage on the ocean side, but the galleon was plain to see — her stern cloaked with weed, and sticking up like a broken box. Nearby was a pile of corroded cannonballs, all glued together like a nest of fish eggs. Dockie said the ship had probably come from Peru about four hundred years before, and had fallen over Rongo in the dark. Mummy Ti had a plate from the wreck. It was pewter, with a royal crest. She used it to give the cats their dinner.

Every now and then I popped up to take a breath, but still there was no dolphin to be seen. I sent out mental calls.

'Where are you, I need you, I love you.'

Nothing happened. It occurred to me then that perhaps they had been so disappointed that I had not seemed to want to help them that they didn't like me any more.

But something else answered those thoughts of mine. My head was flooded with a vast kind voice that commanded me to go away, take another path through the sea, for a child was about to enter the world.

At once I remembered the whale I met when with the dolphins — their 'angel'. It would not be she communicating with me but the friend who always accompanies a mother about to give birth. Aunts, they're called, usually elderly fussy whales who go along to carry the newborn child up to the surface to take his first breath, or to help the mother the same way if she becomes weak or ill. Land people forget that whales need air as we do; they can't hold their breath as long as we think. In fact, beavers can hold their breath longer than some whales can.

It was important for the baby to come into a world of peace and quiet, which is why the Aunt was telling me to go somewhere else. Of course, I realised then that was why the dolphins were not about. At the first call from the Aunt, they would have sped out to sea.

I obeyed at once. I knew the mother whale would be in one of Rongo's bays, for she needed warm, rather shallow water for the birth. It was exciting to think that Sif might be lucky enough to see the Aunt come to the surface with the little one. Out into deeper water I swam, away from those western bays. I knew I could not get lost, for now it was not so very far from our city.

Stig had warned me that the seafloor was very land-scapey out there — immense dunes of rubble and sand, and prehistoric lava set into black rumples, like porridge turned to stone. Old gas tunnels from the volcano opened cavernous mouths, sucking currents in and out and occasionally coughing out vast silver bubbles, squashed lopsided by water pressure. Also, that was a place where giant kelp grew.

My scientific curiosity urged me to see all these things, but I swam onwards, sometimes on the surface, some-times below. Close to the shore I caught a glimpse of our dinghy, and Sif and Mr Jacka diving and splashing around it. I slid underwater, and by the time I popped up for air, I was safely around the point, outside another bay. There I spotted two whales rising to the surface, blowing softly, and submerging again. I wondered why these two females were not with a herd, as they should be. Perhaps their kinsfolk had been scattered or mur-dered by one of the many whale chasers in the Pacific. At that time, though there was an amnesty on whaling, no one had been able to enforce it. And besides the chasers, there were poachers and pirates who merci-lessly killed everything that came their way — females, calves, the rare and almost extinct.

If this had happened to the group to which the females belonged there would surely be other survivors. And these survivors, though they might be few, would already be calling for refugees in those expressive, powerful voices that can be heard ten thousand kilometres or more. High, echoing calls, like those of vast birds, followed by all the mysterious sounds that make up their coded speech — blop, blop, BLOPP! Booqueeeepppp! And sweet whistles, and a long moaning bray. One day, I knew, these two cows, and the baby, would be reunited with their own herd.

Suddenly a huge rubbery ribbon slapped itself around my chest. I nearly shot out of the water like a flying-fish before I recognised it as a blade of kelp. I had travelled too far out to sea. The sensible thing was to turn at once towards land and follow the coast to the city as Sif and I always did. But I was curious about the submarine jungle. I'd never seen such a thing. I promised myself I'd just have a peep and then be on my way.

So I sank down as far as I dared. Kelp does not have roots, but powerful anchors or holdfasts on the seafloor. But I could not see them. They were forty metres or more below me, hidden in the violet blue dusk that says: 'Deep, deep. Danger below!'

Stig had commanded me often: 'When the blue appears, go no deeper. The pressure is too great for your miserable blobs of lungs.'

Like a small fish I flitted through that monstrous foliage, for no leaves on earth are longer than kelp leaves. Where the sunlight filtered, they showed cloudy yellow and brown. Nature had arranged that gas-filled bulges in their structure held them upright in the water so they could get light and oxygen near the surface. Because of this, so did the forest's inhabitants — sponges, squids, lobsters, sea snails and little fish that lived like birds in the boughs.

I floated dreamily, watching a shadow rising from the

blue depths, a dark blur. The shark came straight up, almost under my feet, and the disturbance of its arrival tossed me into the kelp. I have to tell this fast, because it must have happened all in the space of a breath, the one I had in my lungs. But it is true that time stretches. Hours and days passed, and left me with a lifetime memory. I hung amongst the leaves hearing my heart lurch back and forth, afraid the shark would hear it too. But it quietly floated there, the faintest curl of its tail flukes keeping it steady. Perhaps it scented me. It was as big and round as a large barrel, and four times longer than I. It was built of gristle and black leather. Its eye was circular darkness surrounded by china white. A fish scuttled by, and lazily the shark took it, the entire jaw coming forward smoothly, out beyond the lips. Like a machine, a machine with an appetite.

I was a nothing, a titbit, sifted down from the sea's surface, hiding with burning lungs amongst the shifting kelp. My only thought was that if I breathed out, the creature would see the bubbles and charge into the kelp after me. But was it a thought? Rather knowledge, handed down from hundreds of generations of sea-people. If I had any choice, it was between drowning where I clung, or shooting up to the surface and being eaten on the way. No, I did no thinking. My whole body and mind were one enormous yell: 'Help me, I'm going to die.'

The pain in my chest was too great to bear. Red lightning shot across my eyeballs; everything seemed red; I knew some part inside me must burst. Then the sea erupted. Something hurtled past me like a black rocket, tearing the waters apart, jerking the kelp from the seafloor, hurling me away into furious cascades, waterspouts, exploding light, roaring air — air that rushed

87

into my body and out again with a whoop. There I lay, limp amongst the limp kelp, muscles wrenched, half-dead, but half-alive also, and not knowing how or why.

Feebly I thought that the shark had indeed attacked me and somehow I had survived. I tried to swim, to flee, but my arms were lead. All I could do was drag myself over a huge hollow stem and collapse in a trance of shock and fatigue.

While I lay there, I heard a whale blow, whahhhhhhhh! A shower of fine warm mist descended on me. Laboriously turning my head, I saw the whale nearby, half submerged. I saw the blowhole, a huge black leather dimple, trembling as she breathed; her eye, tucked above the long sweep of her upper jaw; her warty brow; the waves slapping over her peaked spine and dorsal fin if she were a half-tide rock. That whale was keeping an eye on me.

I knew the shark had fled. The whale had heard my mind shrieking for help and had come to my aid. She was the Aunt — I recognised her by a barnacle as big as a dinner plate on her upper lip. It must have been painful. Weakly I thought: 'Stig will get that off for you.'

She moved nearer. Perhaps she was curious about the little creature, so ill-shaped, so unskilled in the sea. Beneath me I saw the long winglike flipper, the scalloped edge, the white dents of old wounds and barnacle sores. Shakily I reached out to touch it, and it was warm like a paw, or my own hand. Tears rushed out of my eyes.

I can't describe what love rushed out of me with those tears. I wanted everything that was good for that old whale — a long life, wide wanderings in sweet seas, no wicked ship sneaking up on her to send an exploding harpoon into her guts to blow heart and lungs to pulp.

'I wish I could make it different for you, for all the whales!' I thought, and the answer came in the dolphins' word, in Dockie's — shah, shah, be at peace, little child.

I thought then of the infant whale she must have recently seen born, and she gave me a picture of the small creature, floating belly up, its mother going around it in mournful circles. Somehow I was not surprised to know it had been born dead.

Shock is very strange. In a kind of way a shocked person is asleep, for when I awakened — if awaken I did — the whale was gone, and I was surrounded and supported by dolphins. She must have called them in from the ocean, knowing that she could not take me into the shallow water where I would be safe. They passed me from one to the other, whistling shrilly; sometimes I lay across a back, other times I held to a warm strong tail. At one moment, I know, I rode my friend Emere, for Sif later told me that is what they saw when she and Henry, having heard the furious commotion of the whale's attack on the shark, rowed around the point of the bay.

'The sea was boiling with dolphins,' Sif said. 'I've never seen so many in one place. They pushed you up into the shallows with their snouts. I thought one or two of them might well have stranded. But the queerest thing of all was that there was a whale out in the deep water, lying still as a reef, as if she were watching. Then up came her tail and she dived.'

As Henry and Sif ran the dinghy up the sand, and jumped to help me, the dolphins fled to deep water and stood on their tails in the way they have, creaking anxiously. I tottered to my feet like a rickety cat and fell into Henry's arms. It was the safest, most comforting place I had been for years.

'Hold me, hold me, Henry,' I chattered. 'A shark, I almost drowned, I was going to die.'

And he did. They put me to bed, and Dockie, who had recovered, poured some brandy down my throat. I think I must have been drunk, for I had hideous danger dreams — wandering forever in the brown tangle of kelp, unable to find my way out. And shark's eyes, expressionless and deadly. I expected teeth, tall as fences. But the eyes were more frightening. I shrieked my head off. But even at the worst times I seemed to know that Sif and Henry were with me, ready to save me if things became to bad. All this did not go on for more than a couple of days and nights, for at that age my nervous system was made of refined steel. After that I was ready to talk about my adventure to anyone who would listen.

And I did talk, for as far as Henry Jacka was concerned the jig was up. He now knew not only that we were all the dear friends of whales and other ocean beasts, but that Sif and I were half-seaperson ourselves, daughters of the beautiful merwoman he had seen in the lagoon. It must have been a shock to him. He was after all, a scientist, and things had to be proved fifty times to him (with controls) before he cautiously conceded they might be true. Dockie told me he had taken Henry aside and explained the whole thing. Henry had sat staring into space for three minutes, then rallied.

'Listen here, Dr Copeland,' he had said. 'If civilised human beings live in the depths of the ocean, then I have every sympathy. The topside world's getting wrecked, that's for sure. Who wouldn't opt out of it? But I don't want to speak of it now. I have to think.'

Dockie must have been worried. He was, after all, putting his friends' safety into Henry's hands. But

Mummy Ti had seen that the young man was to be trusted, and so he was. He kept our secret as we had kept it for thousands of years. He did not do this just for Sif's sake. He was an honourable person.

I think I knew that then. Everything in me wanted to like Henry. But in spite of that good moment on the beach when he took me in his arms and I knew I was safe and alive, I would not let myself give in. No, I said to myself sternly, I will not like him. He wants Sif, and I want her too. *And I had her first.* For Sif's sake I decided I would be civil to him, but I would not like him, no matter what.

After he had given me a scolding for swimming off alone, Dockie listened to my reasons. And of course I found out that he had known for a long time that the dolphins were being affected by the tainted sea. Their young ones did not live, or were not born at all.

'Stig and I have had discussions,' he said. 'But what can a man like myself do about it except write letters of protest to the Governments of Pacific countries?'

'But you're an adult!' I cried. What I meant was that he was one of those who ruled the world, who arranged things for the children, pushed them here and carried them there, told them to do this and that — one of the lords of the earth.

'There must be something you can do!' I cried.

'Ah, lass,' he said sadly. 'I'm nothing more than an old drunk on a little island no one has ever heard of.'

But what I felt was anger with him and all the other grown people who hung around like wet dishcloths and let dreadful things happen to our planet.

In spite of my anger I was not sad. I was on that high that comes to people who've had a narrow escape from death, worrying about nothing; blissful, I suppose, that they can breathe and will live to breathe some more. I wrote to Joanne and James, confessing I'd been unfair and unkind, and asking Jo please to reconsider her decision and take me back, since I could never complete my education without her help. I even printed a little letter to Travis, saying his grandmother was happy she had a boy like him in the family. Dockie read my letters. He took them away to post, and I daresay he added some words of his own.

I gave Mr Jacka back his notebook as well.

'Did you find it interesting?' he asked. He was a cool person, but so was I.

'Very,' I said.

'How am I on sea cucumbers?'

'You don't really feel at one with them,' I said politely.

Sif must have told him that I was particularly interested in bêche-de-mer, and other wormy things. This conversation made me feel worse about reading his notebook than I would have done if he'd trounced me about it.

'I expect you got it back from the boys,' he said. 'I'm much obliged, Riko.'

'You're welcome,' I muttered. The menehune were none of his business. Nevertheless, I had a crazy impulse to tell him about them as well. I longed to share things with him — all the wonderful things that made our life on Rongo so good. I had to remind myself he was the enemy. I had to keep on reminding myself, and it almost drove me off the wall. Perhaps it was because he was interested in so many things which interested me.

'I was wondering,' he said, 'if I could have a look at your fishing knife.'

As it was lying on the dressing table I could scarcely say no. While he turned it over and over, tested its

92

balance and weight, I pretended to take no interest. He took a little glass from his pocket, screwed it in his eye, and examined the handle, which was grooved with the sacred galaxy sign, which some races call *swastika*.

'It's very old,' he said at last. 'I think the handle is some kind of tooth. This knife really should be in a museum, you know, Riko. Where did you find it?'

'In the bush somewhere.'

'Would you sell it to me?'

That scared me a little. I decided I must get that knife back to Pig before Henry became even more curious. And until I did manage to return it, I would wear it myself, every waking moment.

Now I turned my stern black gaze on him and said severely:

'Certainly not. It's my fishing knife and I like it.'

He did not argue, but put the knife back and came to sit beside me.

'Tell me about the whale, Riko,' he said. I told him how I had cried out in my mind for help, and she had come.

'Do you think whales have a special feeling for human beings, as dolphins seem to?'

I had to tell him I didn't. Whales are so far beyond us in their intelligence, and manner of living, that I think mankind is very insignificant to them. They have a kindly disregard, they would never hurt us, but they aren't interested in us, either.

'When that Auntie whale came to help me,' I explained, 'to her it would be like lifting a butterfly out of the way, or rescuing a little bird tangled in a big spiderweb. Nothing important. Just kind.'

'I see,' he said, going away.

93

And I knew he really did see. Those were strange days for me. I suppose you could say that I watched love growing between Sif and Henry. Of course I had seen love before. As the youngest girl in my class, I had often watched calf love afflict the older girls — the pain, the tears, the bliss, the weird things they did to make it come true, to make the boy love them too. I had seen fat girls become thin and ill, and slim ones suddenly begin stuffing themselves with potato crisps and other gunk. We had girls who broke into stars' rooms and were thrown out and even arrested. We had an attempted suicide, though the kids all knew it was a fake. That was one kind of love, but what was developing between Sif and Henry was another. Warm and bright, like a marvellous morning when the Island is the whole world and the whole world is blue and green and full of golden light.

They invited me into that world of theirs, they truly did.

'Come on, Riko! Get your gear. We're going fishing, or shelling, or swimming.'

But I said I preferred fooling around in the jungle or the lagoon. And in a kind of way I did. I was so happy in those days. Sometimes it occurred to me that the high I was riding might not last. I was scared that the jealousy and anger of my first days on Rongo might come flooding back.

It was a queer time; I couldn't make head nor tail of it. I remembered that adults were always saying, 'Oh, don't worry! You'll feel different when you're older.' Or: 'In three or four years that won't be a problem to you at all.'

When I was younger, say twelve years old, these remarks maddened me. How could a person change? I felt so whole and complete in myself, as solid and well-shaped as an egg. How could I change without that completeness being ruined? The egg being broken, in fact? And did you go on changing once you'd grown up? It seemed to me a terrifying prospect, and I put the whole thing out of my mind.

But now I wasn't sure. I wanted to ask someone about it, someone who wouldn't laugh or even smile, and I thought of Mr Spry. He was used to people confiding their problems and secrets. Maybe he'd even had murders confessed to him. I decided to ask him if being face to face with death did strange psychological things to a girl, so that she grew up quickly and maybe wouldn't mind if the person she loved best went away to America.

This idea seemed good to me, and I set off at once for his house.

In the bicycle shed, Mr Spry was up a ladder. He was examining a large bunch of red bananas, slung on a ceiling hook. In Epiphany kitchens bananas are used a great deal. Green ones are boiled into porridge so solid it will not fall out of an overturned pan. The menehune loved this horrid food, and Mummy Ti often put a slab of it, wrapped in green leaves, out on the verandah at night. The menehune prowled around the village a lot at night, seeing what they could pick up. This does not mean they were thieves; they just annexed.

'No, the rats haven't got at them,' reported Mr Spry with satisfaction. 'They run along the ceiling upside down, you know. Very intelligent beasts, rats.' He arrived safely on the floor. 'I'm ripening them for the menehune. They're building me a bathroom.'

'A stone bathroom?' I asked, shivering. But I knew why. There was plenty of stone everywhere, and the menehune would build for nothing.

The mission bungalow had never had a bathroom.

95

The Church expected its servants to bathe in the lagoon and rinse off at the marble wash-stand in the bedroom. Proudly Mr Spry showed me the new bathroom. He had had the plumber run a pipe from the rain-tank and set up a shower. Around this the menehune were raising their amazing stone walls. The little people work only at night, and are away at the first crack of daylight. They don't use mortar. All the stones are fitted together, and how they do this work with Stone Age tools no one has ever found out. But their work lasts. Some of the platforms and causeways laid down two thousand years ago in the Marquesas and Ponapé are as good as ever. And anyone can see the Hawaiian fish ponds for himself. Long after the Mission bungalow crumbled into splinters and dryrot, the bathroom would stand, as well as the church and jetty and other menehune structures.

'Of course, there are some small drawbacks,' confided Mr Spry. 'Because of their fear of fire, I must put out the kitchen stove, and it's rather cold this time of year, as you know, Erika. And there was one occasion when I absentmindedly lit my pipe. They all went home and didn't come back for a week. Pig has been very good,' he continued. 'A fine lad. I have every hope of a conversion some day.'

He beamed hopefully at me, and I thought how innocent he was. I felt it was not the moment to bother him with my question, so I smiled nicely, praised his new bathroom and went off. I remembered Pig's devotion to Tane, the forest-person, and the moment after realised that I had not seen Pig since I thumped him on the head near the mangrove swamps. Which was worrying, because he must have heard about the shark. Always before, when I had been even a little sick, Pig had left treasures on my windowsill . . . parrot feathers, or coloured leaves in a little bark basket. I decided to go to my secret place.

All kinds of flowers and fruit were heaped at Tane's feet, and the radio lay there as well. I sat with it in my hand, listening to it chirp, and realising what I had done. I had insulted my friend Pig. Mud had seen it all, and no doubt had shamed Pig before his people.

All young people long for a secret friend, one the adults know nothing about. I had had one from the time I was born. No matter how long I had been away from the Island, Pig had not forgotten me. He took up our jokes and our games from where we had left them. No matter if I were bad tempered or tetchy, he liked me. And he wanted to marry me when we grew up. That was sad, but it showed how faithful and loving he was. I had known it was a bad thing to whack a menehune on the head, and yet I had whacked.

'How could I do anything so stupid?' I moaned.

Something mean inside me murmured: 'Big deal. He's only a leftover weirdie from the Stone Age. What does he matter, after all?'

'You shut up!' I gave the inside of my thigh a punishing pinch. From the corner of my eye I saw a dark blue flutter amongst the trees. Pig's torn jeans? Gladly I ran towards it.

'Is that you, Pig? Wait for me, Pig!'

But there was no answer. Tears came into my eyes. I told myself that was because I was still a bit shaky from the shark happening, and perhaps it was. But I knew very well that without Pig I was like a hermit crab without a shell; unknown dangers coming at me from every side. Joanne didn't want me; maybe James was no longer my friend, either. Sif — but I could not bear to think of Sif. I scuttled away through the dim green tunnel, and burst into the sunshine. But it was just as lonely there as anywhere else.

Mr Jacka came to dinner that night. Dockie was right back in form, the cultured old medico. He'd had a great European education, and could keep pace with Henry on all kinds of subjects. For the first time I heard why such a well-qualified man had left the professional world to settle amongst a green sprinkle of islands in the South Pacific. He had been studying tropical diseases in Tahiti, had taken out a sailboat one weekend, and was blown away.

That was the way many of the great Polynesian voyages of discovery had begun, he said, criss-crossing the vast Pacific, and indeed other seas before that. The brown tribes were born seamen and navigators. They had come from the Land Between the Rivers — the rivers Tigris and Euphrates. They called that mother country Uru, but later people called it Ur.

When they left Uru, they sailed down the Persian Gulf and the Gulf of Oman until they saw India on the eastern horizon. For many centuries they dwelt in India, which its original people named Vrihia. But the wanderers could not pronounce that word. They called the country Irihia.

Driven out at last, they took to the sea and came to Indonesia, a rich scatter of tropical islands. But they were a restless people, moving east from island to island until at last they burst into the Pacific.

So you see it was all right for them. They were master sailors. They knew the stars, currents, winds, birds. But Dockie was a stranger from the northern hemisphere. To be lost on the ocean must have been like the end of the world for him.

'During the night I decided there was no hope for me,' he said. 'I said my prayers, I'm telling you. I lashed everything tight and went to sleep. When I came to myself again it was sunrise, and I found myself amongst a hundred islands — bonny white beaches and coconut palms, and the sea glittering like mica.'

He didn't say why he had left Tahiti and taken the job of Medical Officer in the Epiphanies, but we knew Mummy Ti had a great deal to do with it.

He changed the subject to tell us that he had had a word with Stig. Sif and I and Henry were to visit the undersea city early next day. I sneaked a look sideways at Henry. He had the dazzled look of a person thrilled beyond words, and yet not believing he was really experiencing what he thought he was. Of course, many landpeople had visited the submarine colony through the years — my father, for instance, and quite often the Rong'ans. Dockie had not, for he was a feeble swimmer, and age had made him feebler. Henry was the first scientist. He was still talking excitedly about it when I went off to bed.

Because of the early expedition to the city, by midnight everyone was asleep. I slipped out quietly. I wanted to see Pig and get things straight. There was a clear moon, a few cats out mothing, and owls calling from the mountain darkness. As I approached Mr Spry's bungalow, I felt the air vibrate with a deep humming sound. It was the menehune chanting as they worked.

Building has some kind of religious meaning to these people who themselves live in holes like rabbits. It is a serious thing to spy on them — enough to make them pack up and leave an island all in a night. Still, curious people have spied. The Hawaiian tradition is that they pass the stones from hand to hand so rapidly the walls rise in a twinkling. One tale says that their magic men can make heavy stones float in the air, and another describes how the stones are treated with a certain powerful plant sap, so that they half-melt together, and so do not need mortar.

Certainly I was not going to spy, for I wanted to do nothing more to offend the menehune. My plan was to hide in the dark orchard and call Pig. But there was such a host of the little men, nearly naked, glistening with sweat in the moonlight! I had not dreamed there were so many on Rongo. I turned my face away, and listened to their chant, half in a Polynesian dialect, half in what they called grandfather language, of which I knew nothing. If the missionary could have translated it he wouldn't have been optimistic of conversion. One line I understood, melodious with many rich vowels.

Ka mihi nga mea katoa i konei ki a Rangi, ki a Papa!

which means 'Now all things greet the Sky Father and the Earth Mother' and no doubt referred to Mr Spry's new bathroom. But I thought that those gods would generously bless Mr Spry's soaping and splashings.

'Pig!' I called, and gave a whistle signal we had used in our childhood. Immediately there was a stampede. Flat on my face in the grass, I felt the wind of their passing, and smelt their sweat and body-paint as they crowded past me. When I dared look up, there was nothing to be seen but a pile of worked stones and the almost completed bathroom. And Pig, standing there, looking at me. Seeing me too, for menehune see very well in darkness.

'I didn't look, Pig,' I said. 'I kept to the rule.'

He nodded, and ran off, with me after him, beseeching: 'Wait for me, Pig. I want to say I'm sorry. For hitting you on the head, Pig. It was an awful thing to do.'

So we ran on, me panting and babbling, Pig not saying a word, but rushing along the narrow moonlit tracks with the swift menehune movement that allows them to flicker away to one side or the other in a magical-seeming disappearance. Animal magic it is, of course, the same thing that permits a crab to become a weedy rock, or a stoat to swim into yellow grass and vanish in front of your eyes.

And at last Pig did vanish, and I was alone in the moonlight. There was the huge hahhhhhh! of a waterfall somewhere below me, and above me the crater breathing out ghostly wisps of steam. We were far from the village, on the lee side of the Island.

I knew it, for I knew all of Rongo. Nobody lived on the lee side, for the land was ruined by ancient lava-flows, and there was a big break in the reef, so that heavy seas pounded in and made fishing scanty and dangerous. Winds harried it, too, and what trees there were hunched close to the ground. Even the sea looked cold, a sheet of mercury. I sat down to regain my breath, telling myself I didn't care about Pig or anyone else. It was a long walk home, and my legs felt as if they were dropping off.

A hand touched me.

'Go away!' I said.

'Riko look up.'

So I did. He seemed blurry, through the tears or sweat or whatever it was that bothered my eyes.

'I'm really sorry I hit you on the head, Pig,' I said. 'I know what it means to menehune.'

'That old rubbish!' he said disdainfully. 'I don't believe in that old man stuff. Me and Mud up to date.'

'Then why have you been angry with me?'

He kicked the pebbles around with a horny dark foot, and with splayed toes picked up a white one and pretended to examine it.

'Quit that, Pig! You were furious! I haven't seen you for ages. And you didn't take the radio, either. Why?'

He hesitated for a moment or two. Then he said: 'You come, Riko. I show you something.'

I lumbered myself up and went after him. We turned into the wind, on the downward slope.

'Where are we going?'

But he glided ahead of me like a shadow, and did not answer. The land had become very wild, a jumble of fantastic rocks, black and sharp, piled at the foot of crags furred with jungle. At their base lay a little sliver of a creek. I knew it, though not with interest, for it was too shallow for fish. Pig splashed across. On the other side was a narrow beach scattered with bleached freshwater shells.

I felt a little nervous.

'What is this place, Pig?'

'You not know it, Riko. No one know it but our people.'

Then I saw a short flight of stone steps cut into the cliff face. I followed Pig. In the cliff was a doorway, high enough for a menehune or a child, and darkness beyond. Astonished and alarmed, I hung back, but Pig took me by the hand.

I stumbled after him. The steps went up and then down. Daylight must have entered this place, for twigs pricked my legs, and I could smell the sharp freshness of leaves. The rock under my bare soles was dry and gritty.

Suddenly things began to take shape, dusky shapes of rockfalls; Pig, walking ahead of me, seeing so much better than I. The track hooked around a bend, and light descended upon us. I say descended because that is the right word. Into the fabulous cave, this secret chamber, the moonlight flooded down from a shattered cathedral roof, far, far above.

'It come out high up on mountain,' said Pig. The light was magnified by the white walls of the grotto, and thrown back again and again by a pool filling the entire floor of the cave.

'Fresh water,' said Pig. 'Very soft, like dew.'

We stood on a ledge above this fairy looking-glass.

'Watch.'

Pig dived. The echoes of the splash ran sweetly up the precipitous walls, and so did the light, shattering, reflecting, both dim and bright. When the water calmed I saw Pig's little figure, deep down. I have never seen anything as transparent as that water. Up he came, a brown frog. He shook his fuzzy head, the drops flew out like diamonds, and the hair looked dry once more.

'I never dreamed,' I stammered. 'I don't think anyone on Rongo knows about this cave.'

'It is menehune place,' said Pig. 'Our ancestors who came down starpath found it and made it Tane place. I bring you here, Riko, because you too are loving child of Tane.'

We sat in silence. His hard hand held mine. I was very comfortable, contented.

'You *were* angry when I hit you on the head, weren't you, Pig?'

He nodded. 'Pig not up to date,' he said mournfully. 'Jeans not magic enough to change menehune into groovy guy.'

'What's the matter with being a menehune?' I protested. 'Anyway, I wish I hadn't hit you. Truly, Pig.'

He nodded again and squeezed my hand. I looked around me as if in a dream. The grotto was indeed Tane's place. I recognised the same radiant fatherly presence that dwelt in my secret clearing.

It was not a limestone cave. There were no stalactites. I could see no inlet or outlet to the pool. The only sound of water was the pink-pank of a drip from the ledges. The air was not chilly or dank, but warm and lively, as if full of oxygen. The moonlight picked out long sparkling streaks, perhaps of quartz, in the walls.

'I bring you here special,' began Pig. He stopped and tried again. My skin prickled. I felt something was wrong. 'I bring you to a holy place to say goodbye.'

For a frightful moment I thought that maybe it was menehune law that a person who had his head shamed must eat poison berries or throw himself in the crater of the volcano.

'Goodbye?' I squawked. He looked at me with surprise, and my thoughts became more sensible. 'You're . . . you're going away? The menehune are leaving Rongo?'

'Why we go away?' He was bewildered. '*You* go away.'

'Me?'

'That is why I so upset, because you did not say. Why my Riko do this to me, I ask myself. We are friends since always. Yes, very upset, tears in eyes, not up to date at all. Axe and other menehune sad too, because you and Sif our dear friends. Friends should be told when other friends go away.'

'Do you mean when I go back to school?' I asked, groping for some sense. 'Because I mightn't be going after all. And Sif is staying on Rongo, you know. I told you that before.'

But now we were staring at each other in bewilderment.

'But all seapeople going,' he said doubtfully.

'WHAT?'

The echoes from my yelp went wha-wha-wha all the way up the grotto walls, and probably burst out the top and scared the owls.

I don't know how the menehune seemed to know so much about both land and seapeople. I asked Axe once how it happened, and he said, 'We hear it in air.' But they were always right. I quavered: 'But why? And where are they going? You must have it wrong, Pig.'

'All seapeople go away,' he repeated. 'Too many explosions underwater, many years now.'

'Do you mean the nuclear experiments in the Pacific?'

Pig nodded. 'Water poisoned, fish dying, big cracks on bottom of sea. You ask your brother Stig.'

'But where would they go?'

'Far far away. Little island called Kopu. In cold waters.'

I had never heard of it, but instantly I imagined it, its forests dark and crabby, full of mist and bogs. Grey curdly seas, and ice floes clashing along the reef. But would there be a reef? Corals could not grow in such cold. I let out a snort of grief and horror, and Pig put my head on his chest and patted it sympathetically.

'How could they live there? It sounds awful!'

'They must leave Epiphanies. Too dangerous now. Whales and dolphins and seapeople, all get sick.'

It was what I had thought myself, and yet now that I was brought up against a solution to the problem, I thought I would die. Why hadn't Dockie told me when we spoke about the danger to the dolphins and whales?

And Sif, if she too knew — for the first time she had kept a secret from me. I was on the outside of everything. The city abandoned! Stig, Matira, everyone going far away. The undersea city would be left, as others had been left, to the octopuses and sea-stars.

'Everyone go,' said Pig, stroking my hair. His chest smelt a bit fishy but it was warm, a boy's hard chest. A mysterious something that had drowsed behind my waking thoughts, stirred sweetly. I had a dim understanding of how Sif felt about Henry. Confused, I pulled back.

'I can't go with them, Pig,' I said. I explained about my land half, how it was stronger than my seapeople half. My lungs weren't right. My blood was second-grade.

Pig jumped up and did a little war dance on the ledge. He toppled over backwards into the pool. There he frolicked like a porpoise, yelling: 'Riko not going away! Riko not going away!'

The echoes were so fierce I had to put my hands over my ears. He clambered out and hugged me, wetting me to the skin.

'Why Riko not happy too? You want to go away to horrible Kopu?'

'I don't want anyone to go!' I wailed.

'Come on, I take you home,' he said. On the way I tried to explain.

'I don't want to be left without a family, you see. I never saw much of Stig and Matira and the others, but I always knew they were there. I just had to come back to Rongo and there they'd be. It was the same for Sif. But when they are all far, far away I'll never see them, maybe for years. Maybe never. I have to go to school and University, I'll have to work. I'm a land person, and I can't change that.'

'You marry me and be menehune,' suggested Pig hopefully.

'You know very well I'm too huge,' I said, and began to blubber.

I remember that calm moonlit night was full of little tremors; twitches of the earth's hide that made the sea gasp in its regular rhythm, the drowsy birds faintly squeak in protest. But Pig and I were used to shakes. They meant nothing to us. At the time I had a doleful idea that this uneasiness of the earth merely echoed the agitation in my mind.

Just before he left me, Pig took me by the shoulders and gave me the nose-rub which means 'You're family. I'm family.' It was a great honour. But I was too distracted to pay attention. Only a few weeks before I had been the luckiest person in the world. But now there seemed to be no place for me.

I sneaked into my bed, but was unable to sleep. My head was like a beehive. I heard my sister softly breathing and wondered whether she really did know what the seapeople planned to do. I didn't think so. She had the kind of face that can hide nothing.

Dawn came, a sudden rattle of the waves, a pink haze along the skyline. Through the torn banners of the banana grove, I saw Venus — Kopu, as we call it — burning like a faraway campfire. The island Kopu must also be in the east, under that planet, over towards South America.

'South America!' I groaned, for it seemed a million kilometres away. My chest ached, I couldn't breathe. I wondered if it would be all right if I woke up Mummy Ti to have a talk. I longed for someone to hug me and understand what I was feeling. Thinking of this, I fell asleep, but had slept only a short while when Sif awakened me.

107

'Come on, sleepyhead,' she sang. 'Don't you remember? Today we're going to show Henry our city!'

She was so excited and pleased I understood at once that she knew nothing about the migration to that wintry island far away.

Chapter 6

I knew I had to tell Sif; it wouldn't be fair to let her reach the city and find out by chance. I didn't want her to feel the way I had felt since I heard Pig's news, afraid, half-sick, and unable to think straight. But I did not know how to handle the problem of telling her. The more I thought about it, the more certain I was that Stig had expected Dockie to tell us the evening before. But he hadn't. And neither had Mummy Ti. How could they be so cruel to us?

For the first time in my life I would have been quite pleased to be back in Lindfield, with Joanne scolding Travis, Giselle slopping milk — ordinary, safe.

I strapped on Pig's knife, which I had forgotten to return to him, so distracting had been our night in the moonlight. It had, anyway, become a sort of good luck piece to me, reminding me always of my faithful friend.

Sif put her head around the bathroom door. 'Get a move on, Riko!'

'Sif!' I called after her. 'I have to speak to you about something . . .'

'Henry's waiting down at the jetty,' floated back her voice. 'Do hurry, Riko!'

If only she had come back then! If only I had run after her at that moment and told her, not for her sake but for my own, because I needed a friend to share my lonely fear.

Instead I felt so desperate about everything and every-one that I barged into Dockie's room, full of fire. He put down his early morning cup of tea with a jerky hand. I could see by his baleful red eyes he'd been at the schnapps the night before.

'Why didn't you tell me and Sif about the family going away!'

'Oh, losh!' he groaned. He pulled the sheet over his head and I pulled it off.

'How did you find out?'

'The menehune.'

'Those stumpy wee devils know everything. A pity they don't keep their traps shut.'

'Why didn't you tell me, Dockie? I'm not a baby. You must have known for ages.'

'I didn't think it would be so soon,' he confessed. 'I thought you'd be away back to school, and that it would be easier to write and tell you then.'

'Dockie,' I exploded. 'That's lousy. I never thought you'd squib anything.'

'It's being old,' he said mournfully. 'Aye, I thought there'd be plenty of time to let you know. But now Stig says they'll have to move on, and smartly, too. Bad things have been happening in the ocean. You wouldn't go too far if you called it an emergency.' He sighed deeply. 'Also, Stig says this is the best month for the eastward current.'

'And you didn't even tell Sif?'

He shook his head, looking sheepish. To my dismay I felt my chest tighten, my throat begin to close up. If I didn't get out of there I would begin to bawl, and prove to Dockie I was a baby after all. Into the silence came Dockie's ashamed voice: 'I couldn't bring myself to it, when it came to the point. A dozen times I had my mouth open to tell you both, but when I thought of Sif leaving with the rest of them, the words stuck in my gizzard.'

It had never occurred to me that Sif might want to go with Mother and Stig, even though she was not very much like me. She was a true seaperson. Also she loved Stig and Mother and the others even more dearly than I did.

'She wouldn't leave *me*!' I cried. But Dockie shook his head dolefully.

'All said and done, she belongs to the sea and them that live in it. She'll go back to them, lass. It's her nature. Ah, a man takes a devil of a risk when he allows himself to get fond of anyone.'

He put the sheet over his face again, and this time I didn't pull it off. Just outside the door I found Mummy Ti. She had been listening, for she gave a heartbroken sniff.

'*You* didn't tell us either!' I accused.

She shook her head dolefully. 'Oh, darlen, Dockie say he do it for sure. But then he get so upset about the people leaving Rongo, he drink too much. He so old, darlen — how he ever going to get to Kopu to see his friends again?'

'Then you should have told us. It's not fair!'

Two tears rolled down her cheeks, so I had to put my arms around her as far as they would go, and pet her a little. Though I loved Matira, that was a different love from what I felt for Mummy Ti. Mummy Ti had brought me up, loved me without reservation, forgiven me everything. Sometimes when I was little, and my mother had asked that I spend a few days with her in the undersea city, Mummy Ti had not said a word of protest. But always, when I was brought back, she was there waiting on the sand to catch a first glimpse of me.

111

'There now, Riko,' she said, patting me soothingly. 'You my little child. Mummy Ti never let bad things happen to Riko.'

But I felt bad things had already happened, and choked out: 'Dockie thinks Sif will go away too!'

'M'm, m'm,' she said reflectively, and then, with a twinkle of mischief. 'I been wondering what young Henry say about that. Eh? You wonder, too, Riko?'

Well, I hadn't thought of that either. My heart filled with hope. Mummy Ti, still looking mischievous, gave me a push.

'Go on, Riko, you tell Sif yourself about mother and brother going away. Sister best to tell, anyway.' She raised her voice to a small shout. 'Better than silly old dog's bone!'

She must have been truly upset about Dockie's cowardice.

As I tore down to the jetty I heard the outboard motor cluck into action. It had been arranged that one of the Island boys should take us out into deep water, mainly for Henry's sake, as he was no long-distance swimmer. I had ideas of calling my sister off the boat and calmly and tenderly breaking the bad news to her.

But as soon as she spotted me, she cast off. She was jumping up and down with impatience, asking what was the matter with me, I knew perfectly well we had planned to leave before sunrise. She wore a blue bikini with a lighter blue shirt over it, her hair loose. She loved to feel it wafting around in the water. She looked so beautiful I almost missed my leap into the boat. Of course the Islander was deliberately edging it away from the jetty, just to tease me.

So I missed that chance as well. With an asthmatic snarl we bumped away over the glassy water. The noise

112

made any conversation impossible. The Islanders love to be rough with motors, and this one had a lot of rust anyway. I couldn't even ask what was the matter with Henry. He was hunched up in the bow looking as though he wasn't enjoying anything. I thought he might be one of the seasick sort, but later on he told me he was as nervous as a cat at the thought of meeting real mermaids at last. He wore scuba gear, though Sif and I had told him no more than swim shorts were necessary, and goggles, if he liked. But I suppose he felt more comfortable in all that Loch Ness monster stuff. He was even wearing flippers. He had great legs, though, muscular and brown.

Sif went forward to sit with him, smiling and talking right into his helmeted ear. She took his hand and put it for a moment against her cheek. I had a pang when I saw how her touch made him smile and relax. I didn't want her to waste her time comforting a Loch Ness monster; I wanted to be telling her about the seapeople, and how frightened I was, and Sif putting her arm around me and saying it didn't matter at all as long as we had each other.

As the boat slowed and circled to a halt, I flopped over the side, feeling deserted. When I rose for a breath, Sif and Henry were both in the water. They waved and dived. The Island boy grinned at me knowingly: 'Your turn one of these days, ol' Riko! You so jealous you nearly break your face!'

I uttered a suitable growl and duck-flipped over into the chill depths. But I hadn't taken the right kind of breath, and with scalding chest returned to the surface. The thing was, I wasn't jealous. I had expected, perhaps, that all my old feelings of anger and loss would return. But they did not. I did not want anyone to take Sif away from me, but I would much rather have her marry

Henry and live in the States than go away to an island where I might never see her again. That was what Mummy Ti had meant.

Making up my mind not to think any further than that, at least until I told Sif about Kopu, I glanced back at my beloved island. It looked like a dusky dragon, tail curled around its nose, all its horns and spines hidden in daybreak cloud. Having fixed my position, I slid down into the gauzy blue. Henry and my sister were blurry shapes in the distance. Henry marked by a tall cloud of silvery bubbles fizzing from a valve. These bubbles are one reason why the seapeople don't like scuba divers. Fish don't mind bubbles, but they scare off whales and other sea beasts. I glided away then, through a shoal of small fish, hovering asleep with open eyes. The coral was still feeding; the reef rippled and swayed with colourless daisies that sunrise would change in a flash to dazzling yellow and pink.

There is something magic about seawater. Once a person is immersed in it, it is impossible to worry about anything. I even began to feel better about the future of the seapeople. Through thousands of years they had survived strange perils — volcanic eruptions, tidal waves, and, almost worst of all, naval warfare. Depth charges and exploding battleships had sometimes wiped out entire cities. There was also that nightmare time when a meteorite, so large it looked like a little moon, had bellowed down into the Indian Ocean and made the water boil for a week. Those who had escaped the seething sea, sought a new home and founded another city.

So there was still hope, I thought, that the brainless ones who fouled their own food with poisonous chemicals, and were so insane as to tip the worst contaminants known to man into the ocean — which nourished sky

114

and land — would all learn better, or be justly punished by the gods with flood, fire and earthquake. Though those things would kill everyone else as well.

Or maybe they would just die out, those greedy murderers. And it was at that moment I had the faint wisp of an idea how it would happen, how our world would indeed be saved.

The shadow of a big bird, striding over the water's surface in order to get lift, passed above me, and I knew sunrise was close.

Pale blue shimmered through the water. The sea bloomed with colour — golden and grape-green fish, a seabed shark freckled like a foxglove, and hordes of fairy shrimps as clear as glass. Henry's cherry-red air tank caught the eye like a traffic light. He and Sif were playing with a manta ray, a large one. There were dozens of them about. They had been snoozing in piles on the ocean floor.

It unscrolled its flat body, and set sail with a ripple of the winglike edges. Mantas have large brains; the largest amongst the fish. Like most intelligent creatures they are as peaceable as trees. This one didn't mind Sif sitting on its back, scratching and stroking where its neck would have been, if it hadn't been a ray. Henry clung to a big remora or suckerfish that had attached itself to the giant. I couldn't help grinning; he looked as though he were straphanging in a bus.

The pair of them were skylarking, circling around one another, pretending to sink, skimming away at top speed. I realised it was a courting dance. Dolphins and seals do the same thing, and, on land, possums and herons and butterflies.

It was beautiful, too. That mysterious feeling I had experienced when Pig stroked my hair returned, and I even said to myself: 'Your turn one of these days, ol' Riko!'

Every now and then Sif flew up to the surface to take a breath. She did not seem to be able to hold air as long as she used to. Perhaps that cough she couldn't shake off was troubling her.

'I'll ask Stig for rebreathers on the return journey,' I decided. 'Henry might like to try one, too.'

Now, all this time I was aware that somewhere in the ocean whales were gathering. Far out, maybe twenty kilometres offshore, the sea was crowded with whales. I heard nothing, saw nothing, yet my whole mind seemed full of whale thought, swelling and cross-fading into silence. It was strange that so many should suddenly appear, when the mother whale and her friend had seemed to be alone. It was whale time, of course, for having young and playing and singing. Even conferring, as large herds are believed by some experts to do. They have plenty of leisure then, as they do not eat until they turn south to the Pole for the mating season. Then they gorge krill by the tonne.

I sent out an exploratory query or two, but my feeble chirrup would have been lost in that vast submarine chorus.

Ahead of me Henry and my sister trod water. They were face to face with the submarine city but Henry couldn't see it at all. Sif smiled, and I was grinning as well. All sea things that feel themselves defenceless try to look like something else. Everyone knows about hermit crabs, and fish that pretend to be stones, and molluscs that grow gardens on their backs. So sea cities mostly look like reefs, or the side of a cliff, or a big pile of rocks, not because they are defenceless, but because their citizens discovered ages ago that their land cousins are not only stickybeaks, but like to pull to pieces anything rare and strange.

The Rongo city was built into the sea side of a lava outflow that had solidified in ancient times. Its lifelines ran up into old gas tunnels that were as shiny as black crystal, and full of queer stale mineral smells. One of those tunnels came out in an extinct, fern-filled crater on Rongo's west. The Islanders knew about it; in ancient times they had always taken refuge there when fierce tribes swept over the Island on their way south. It was down that tunnel they had gone, braving the darkness and the mysterious throb and shudder of the volcano, when the seapeople called upon them to help with the building of the city.

To me the city clearly showed its dome, its stumpy towers and mooring masts. But to Henry it seemed nothing but a cliff hidden in marine growth. Gently, Sif parted the weed that coiled and dodged this way and that. Immediately the airlock sprang open and light steamed out, catching Henry and my sister as if in the beam of a searchlight.

Ordinarily this would not have happened, but Stig loved to be dramatic. His great bare arm shot out. He hauled Henry into the outer lock. Sif and I followed close behind. There was the sound of a gurgling drain as the water cleared out of the lock, and we could breathe fresh air.

Henry took out his mouthpiece and removed his mask. Stig roared with delight at his visitor's dumbfounded look. He pressed a control. With a faint pop the inner door opened, and we stepped into light and warmth.

'Welcome!' boomed Stig. He hugged Sif and myself,

117

then smacked down his webbed hand on Henry's shoulder. Henry looked at the hand with close attention. I could just imagine the pages that would be filled in the yellow spiral notebook that evening. Then he glanced down at my brother's mighty legs. He didn't actually burst out with 'You've got feet!' but I could read it on his face.

Anyone else would have looked at the buildings, stacked in cells like a honeycomb, each cell ornamented with pearlshell, or silver, or gems according to the fancy of its owner. The one closest to Henry blazed with emeralds. Our brother Fredrik had salvaged them from the galleon where eventually he lost his life. But no, Henry was a scientist. Emeralds were emeralds no matter where he saw them. A man with a webbed hand was another thing altogether.

The first thing Henry said was a wondering: 'But it's warm in here!' Then he gave Stig a sheepish but cheerful grin, as though to acknowledge that any race with the technology to build a city under the sea knew very well how to keep it at a comfortable temperature. Stig gave another bellow. He really relished Henry.

The city was not in disarray, but from the corner of my eye I could see the signs of departure — bales and containers ready to be loaded, a workman on the roof of the Assembly chamber carefully levering up the gold tiles. I knew then that telling Sif about the migration could not wait.

I tugged at the tail of her wet shirt. 'Sif, I have to speak to you. Please, Sif.'

'Oh, Riko! Right this minute?'

She wanted to watch Stig and Henry getting along like old friends. She had longed for them to like each other, and so they did.

118

'Sif! Please listen.'

I didn't want Henry to hear. Sif could tell him in her own good time. Also, in a kind of way, I didn't want Stig to know that his friend Dockie had let him down. The pair of them were intently examining the inside of the airlock; already a flock of children had gathered around them.

'What's the matter, Riko?'

I rushed out with it. 'They're all leaving, Stig and Matira and everyone. Very soon, Sif. To a little island near South America!'

Sif said not a word; she just turned as white as paper.

'Sif, do you understand? Dockie was supposed to tell us, but he didn't. Look around, Sif, can't you see they're getting ready?'

She looked around them, slowly as in a dream, and noticed what I had observed. Then she whispered: 'Matira!'

She began to run towards Matira's house. I thought it might be best if she went alone. Matira was with Sif longer than she was with me — nearly eight years. But I did long to go as well.

I looked around then and saw Henry almost submerged under all those children. If he had never seen seachildren before, they had never touched and spoken to a live scuba diver. They knew all about such monsters from television, which was their chief means of observation of the upper world. And some, the older ones, had been daring enough to swim to the lagoon to watch and giggle at the tourists spearfishing in the safe waters.

The children were as inquisitive as menehune and much cheekier. There was such a commotion of laughter and squealing, such a patting and tugging, that at last

119

Stig pulled away the kids and sent Henry to his own house to remove his heavy gear before his admirers damaged a zipper or pulled off a strap. Then Stig looked around for me and saw me standing alone.

For some reason I thought he might be vexed with me. He was so large, a Viking, and though I loved him, I was in awe of him. I stuttered out how I'd tried and failed to tell Sif until now, and how upset she'd been, looking as if she were going to faint. His strong hand took me by the back of the neck. I don't know what I expected. He shook me gently to and fro and rumbled, 'And you too are upset, my little fish?'

It was the first time anyone had asked me that. Pig had been glad I couldn't go with my family because he didn't want to lose me. Dockie had been brokenhearted because he wouldn't see his old friends ever again. Mummy Ti had said some useful things but none about me being left alone, an orphan, really. And I didn't know how Sif felt about it. Not yet, anyway.

'Don't go, Stig! Don't go!' I wailed. Stig picked me up like a puppy and hugged me. Even though I could scarcely breathe I felt safer than I had for weeks. But the soreness in my heart had to burst out, and it did: 'I might never see you again, Stig!'

He just hugged me tighter.

'You know why we're going, Riko?' I nodded but he explained more clearly how, since the 1980s when the industrial nations had begun to burrow down into the ocean floor, mining for cobalt and manganese from Hawaii to Samoa, huge cracks had appeared far from the blasting area. Poisonous gas had squeezed out and killed vegetation for thousands of hectares around. Most of the plantations where the seapeople harvested their food were ruined already.

120

'Down in the deeps,' said Stig 'magma is welling out of crevasses I've never seen before. There's a strange bulge forming between Rongo and Big Island; perhaps the volcano is becoming active once more. And the whales — they say the deep water is getting hotter.' He broke off, shook his head soberly. 'All that and more, Erika. So we must flee to safer waters before we are overwhelmed.'

I wept then. Although I knew the tribe's decision must have been final, it had not sounded so until my brother Stig rumbled it out.

'Maybe I could come with you, after all, Stig! I don't mean now, or by water, because I'm not made right for that. But when you're settled, maybe I could fly to Kopu, or travel by ship?'

He put me down then, still holding my hands and looking into my eyes. 'No, Riko, you have other things to do. We need friends on land, people who know all about us, and yet would never destroy us. People with learning and intelligence like Henry — and you, when you are older.'

'And Sif too?' I wanted to hear him say that she would be staying.

'Maybe Sif, too. We must wait and see.'

'Oh, Stig! Why have you chosen Kopu? It sounds such a miserable dump,' I lamented.

'Yes,' he said, 'a poor, windswept place, which is why no one wants to mine it, or build a nuclear reactor there, or even remember it exists. So for a while it will be safe for us.'

He told me that for three years now they had sent out scouts, and this island Kopu seemed the best for them. Strangely, a sea city had once existed there, in time beyond legend, and then abandoned. Perhaps that prehistoric tribe had not been able to endure the freezing winters, said Stig.

'But we must be tougher. When times are hard, only the tough survive. And I say that to you, too. I rely on you, Riko. So, no more tears.'

I knew what he meant. He was my brother, and in many ways I was like him.

'And now, here comes Henry. You must show him our city, little fish.'

'I want to see if Sif is all right,' I protested. 'I want to see Mother, too.'

'Do as I say. Better for me to see Sif.'

I threw my arms around him. They went about as far as they did around Mummy Ti. But Stig was all muscle and golden hair, so it was rather like hugging a lion. I thought he looked like Poseidon, though I rather think that ocean god had blue hair, like our own Pacific guardian, Tangaroa, who is Tane's relative.

Henry now wore his swim shorts and a bright piece of cloth twisted around his middle as a kilt. That was Pacific merman fashion, unless they were wearing tails. He looked disappointed that Sif wasn't to be his guide, but I explained that she'd gone off to see Mother first.

I felt very unhappy, but Stig had given me an order, so I tried to concentrate on Henry and the city. The doomed city.

Henry stood with his face upraised. I could see his glance travelling over the dome, down the walls, looking for the source of the soft greenish brilliance that illuminated the city. I dreaded his asking me where it came from, for that was a question no one could answer.

'I don't know, Henry. No one knows. Our people understand how to bring it into their dwellings, that's all. No, it's not electricity or anything like that.'

'What is it then?'

'We call it *te mata*, but that just means "the light" anyway. The earth produces it somehow.'

I told him that the light was just as intense far under the water as it was in the city. (And in the menehune burrows, I could have added, but did not.) That by night each island flashes forth darts and lightnings that can be seen below the sea's surface a hundred and fifty kilometres away. The old navigators had steered by *te mata* on nights when the stars were clouded over. It is known all over the Pacific, and in some island groups is called by beautiful names, such as 'the glory of the ocean'.

'Is it hot?' he asked.

'No. And it can't be used for power. The seapeople get power from another source.'

Henry nodded briskly. Then he sat down on the ground and buried his face in his arms.

'Are you all right, Henry?'

'Yes,' he said. 'My head won't really explode. I just need to rest it for a moment. It's okay for you, Erika, you were born to all this. You'll have to have patience with me.'

I waited for a minute or two. Then he jumped up, as cheerful and enthusiastic as ever.

'Come on! I want to see everything!'

I cannot say, even now, how the city was built, for that technology belongs to the sea tribes and has never yet been used on land. It is their secret. But I can say that submarine cities are always built as part of isolated islands. Island people are different from those who live on continents. It is as if they truly belong to the sea. The island is just a dry place to put their feet and grow their vegetables. The ocean is not just a food supplier, fortress, and a highway to other lands; it is a mighty parent careful of its children. It fattens the clouds that water the gardens and make the forests flourish; it tosses up on the sands careless riches — floating seeds like coconuts, mangrove kernels and useful nuts, as well as oil drums, jetty piles and runaway dinghies.

So it is natural that the seapeople need friendly islanders as support or protection. Intermarriage has never been rare. In the old days defeated chiefs or outcast warriors often took refuge with the sea tribes. For this reason the seapeople always look a little or a lot like their islanders. Matira and her family were brown, with curly black hair. But Irish mermaids, I have heard, are pale as moonlight, with hair so fair it is often thought to be green.

I showed Henry the rustless metal structures that cantilevered the dome into the flank of the Island; the giant pumps, the craftsmen's shops. He was quickwitted and observant and immediately saw which parts had been scavenged from wrecked ships.

'But how did your technicians get such weighty components out of the wrecks and up to this height?'

'We have the equipment.' I was vague about it, not being interested. 'Oh, and we have powerful vehicles, too.'

'What kind of vehicles?'

I took him to one of the glass walls. At least, I call it glass, though it was produced from a different mineral. I meant to show him the skipper usually stationed out there. But to my dismay there was a whole gaggle of them, wagging at the ends of their tethers above the fearful chasm behind the city. They had plainly been made ready for the migration.

Henry looked stunned.

'They're deepsea ships,' I explained.

'But they look just like . . .'

The sight of those ships ready to bear my family away, ready to bear Sif away, was too much for me. My throat began to ache, and I wished Henry would disappear.

'Flying saucers?' he said. I pulled myself together for a moment.

'Come on, Henry! If they're made round and flattish it's because they travel faster under the water that shape. And they can skip along the surface as well, like flying fish. In fact, we call them skippers. But if anyone sees them on the surface, and mistakes them for flying saucers, that's not our fault.'

I suppose my voice faltered, for he looked at me keenly. 'What's the matter, Erika? What's upset you? You've been like a hen on hot bricks since we left home this morning.'

His saying 'home' like that, his kind shortsighted look — these things were the end for me.

'Oh, Henry!' I cried with an awful puppylike yip. 'I don't know what to do!'

'The first thing might be to tell me about it,' he said. So I did. All of it. He listened carefully, which was a credit to him when he was surrounded by so much strangeness, which must have interested him more than I did.

'It's Sif,' I kept saying. 'Please don't let her go away with them, Henry. Please.'

'It's not my place to persuade her, Riko,' he answered after a while. 'Maybe she wants to go with her mother and brother.'

'She won't if you ask her to stay,' I said desperately. I told him how happy Sif had been since he had come to Rongo. I said a great deal about how Sif felt about life, about him.

125

Henry turned aside and examined the doorway behind us, each facet of its octagon decorated with paintings of squid and striped nautilus. Thinking he had lost interest in what I was saying, the way adults often do, I cried in despair: 'You don't care about us at all!'

He came back to me then, looking at me seriously and saying, 'Don't say any more about this, Riko. Not to Sif, and not to me. It doesn't matter what any of us feels about it. Your sister has the right to choose for herself whether she stays or goes away.'

I babbled on, until he said firmly, almost sternly: 'No more, Erika. This is not your business.'

Not my business! My sister not my business! It was just as well that Stig came along before I could say another word.

'I'll take over now, Riko,' he said. 'Matira wants to see you.'

My mother Matira was of chiefly rank. Stig had his importance amongst the seapeople through her. As well, she was a great beauty and, like many beauties, believed the world belonged to her. At quite an early age I had understood that. But Sif felt differently. Belonging more to the sea than I, Sif had the feelings of a young dolphin towards its mother. To infant dolphins their mother is all in all. For a long time they swim above or beside her, copying her every movement, often softly touching her with their flippers to make sure she is still there.

Matira sat now in her big chair, her feeble feet curled under her, pearls glossy amongst the folds of her green garment. One hand idly twisted locks of Sif's hair into curls. She did not seem disturbed by my sister's tears.

'Mother, what have you been saying to Sif?' I demanded, but all I got was her lazy smile and a gesture to sit at her knee.

'I shall need one daughter to come with me to Kopu,' she explained. 'Such a lonely, faraway place! I must have company there. But Johanna is a disappointment, and you, my Rikoriko, are no more than a little scrap of nothing in particular. So Sif shall come with me.'

'Not if she doesn't want to!' I croaked. My voice had turned to a croak because I was a little scared of my mother. When she turned those fathomless black eyes on me I shrivelled, just as people did when I gave them the same stare.

'You mustn't make her go, you mustn't,' I whispered.

Sif looked up then, her face so puffy and red-eyed with tears, her expression the one she used to have when Joanne was hassling her, an expression of 'Help me, help me, I don't know what to say!'

'She doesn't want to go!' I cried.

'What do you know about anything, my darling?' said my mother tenderly, running a finger down my nose. 'You are almost a landcrab. Not that I love you less for that,' she added, with her beautiful smile. 'But Sif belongs to the sea, as Stig and I do, and you don't altogether understand her.'

'I do, I do!' I cried.

'Be quiet now, Rikoriko,' said my mother in her sweet way, meanwhile turning her commanding eyes upon me so that I fell silent.

But I was not going to leave Sif to be persuaded. I sat there, eyes downcast, and listened. It became clear that Matira knew all about Henry, even about Sif's caring for him.

'Dockie, I suppose,' I reflected. 'Blabbermouth. And

127

Stig. Another babbler who never thinks before he speaks.'

Our mother did not chide or reprove Sif. She spoke so lovingly, so gently, in the mermaid's beguiling voice of which we read in the legends. Sif had that voice too.

'My darling,' said Matira. 'I cannot allow you to think of loving a landperson.' She sighed. 'When I see what sorrows and problems I have brought to my own children and grandchildren, I regret that I ever laid eyes on Erik Magnus.'

'But you loved him, you must have loved him,' wailed Sif. My mother seemed to sink into herself, brooding darkly. She rubbed her frail malformed feet as though memory of those years on land made them hurt.

'I loved him at first,' she said. 'But if your father had lived, I would not have gone back to him. The land is no place for a seaperson.'

'But Sif and I are only half seaperson,' I blurted. 'And the land is a lovely place. It's good enough for me, most of the time.'

'I don't wonder about that,' she smiled, and ruffled my hair good-humouredly. I realised for the first time that probably I was a disappointment to her, too, though not as much as Joanne.

'To marry a human brings nothing but trouble,' sighed Matira, 'so, my Sif, you will come to Kopu with me.'

Sif made a great effort, she was so under the spell of that singing, coaxing voice. 'No,' she said. 'I must think about it.'

'There is no thinking,' laughed Matira. 'Run away now, my darling, and begin your preparations for the journey.'

Sif gave a cry as if she had been stabbed. Quickly I took her away, down to the city gardens, where the ocean rushed in and out of the channels, nourishing the plants. Sif had stopped crying. She was cold and white, shivering now and then.

'You do exactly what you want to do, Sif,' I urged.

'I can't choose, I can't,' she whispered.

'Of course you can!' I said stoutly. 'I'll help!'

I said some rough things about Matira's queenly airs, giving us both orders as though she hadn't run away and left us when we were small and needed her.

'If it hadn't been for Mummy Ti, where would we have been? Matira is a spoiled, selfish woman, whether she's a seaperson or not.'

'But she's our mother, Riko.'

'Mummy Ti is our mother! And did you hear all that rubbish she was talking about bringing sorrows on her children and grandchildren because she married a landman! She was as pleased as could be when I told her Travis was born with webbed fingers. She is just playing on your feelings for her, Sif, because she's frightened of going to a strange place and wants help and company.'

Even while I said these things, I felt a small thrill of fear, as though Mother might suddenly appear and punish me. Perhaps, I thought afterwards, the seapeople really were just a little strange to me; I didn't know all their powers. Maybe I was more of a landcrab than I thought. But I turned my mind away from that. I had enough trouble to contend with.

'But I love her, Riko,' Sif whispered.

'So do I,' I answered. 'But loving isn't everything.'

But I knew that for Sif, it was. No matter which way she decided she would lose a person she loved.

'I don't forget,' she said, 'how lonely our father was.'

'I remember, too,' I said, bitterly.

129

'It wasn't her fault,' Sif protested. 'Sometimes people like us get so homesick for the sea, that we just have to go back. I couldn't bear it if . . . I mean, suppose in time I came to feel like that and I . . . oh, Riko, life is so difficult!'

I knew very well what she was thinking. Suppose things did come to marriage between her and Henry (or some other man some day, it didn't really matter) and she had that terrible, undeniable urge to return to the sea. All I could do was to hope it would never happen.

One of the children came to fetch us, for Stig needed us. Sif washed her face in the welling channel, and combed her hair. She put on a kind of calm. I was proud of her, and would have told her so, but her face was so pale and shut up, I could not think of the right words. When Stig came to meet us, she asked: 'Where's Henry?'

'Watching the whales,' he replied. 'They're in a stir about something. Can't you hear them? I'll go out and speak with their old father very soon.'

I could hear the whales in my head, muttering and grumbling. But the pictures I saw were murky and without form, shot through with sudden giddy glimpses into rifts of smoky water, boiling with unrecognisable luminous motes. I could get no sense from these pictures, but they filled me with alarm.

'What can you make of it, Riko?'

I shook my head. 'I don't know, Stig. Nothing clear.'

Sif had left us to find Henry, so I told my brother that Mother was determined to take Sif with her across the ocean, disregarding Sif's own wishes.

'And she said hard things about seapeople mixing with landpeople.'

Stig snorted. 'A lot of nonsense. *I* see nothing wrong with half-breeds. You're one. I'm one. And look at me!'

130

I smiled at his innocent conceit. Certainly he was magnificent whether in feet or tail. I lovingly tugged his whiskers.

'But Sif takes things to heart so, Stig.'

Many of the people crowded along the glass wall, much interested in what must have been for Henry Jacka the strangest sight.

The undersea, shot with sunlight as it was — for the city, as I have said, was close to the surface — was alive with humpback whales. Only four or five had come close to the wall, but beyond them in the misty blue shifted and flitted vast tadpole shapes, for whales in deep water, when they are playing or socialising, tend to stand on their tails, lean over backwards, swim upside down, and indeed do almost anything but swim horizontally.

Henry had his hands over his ears, for near the city wall the noise was almost unbearable. How many whales were singing I could not tell, for they have no vocal organs; no one knows how they speak and sing, so it was impossible to see which ones were conversing with us. Sometimes an observer sees a vocalising whale emit a long stream of bubbles white as suds from the blowhole; other times there is no exhalation. Their voices remain their own mystery.

These whales spoke to us. I heard the bass pipes of an organ, trills, yawning sounds, yodelling, groaning, and many musical magpie notes.

Long afterwards, when Henry Jacka described in a book his first hearing of that marvellous chorus, he said it was 'an alien concerto, swelling out of the depths' instead of down from the stars. And that is exactly right.

But at the time he was stupefied by the size of the whales themselves. He yelled into my ear, 'Giants!

131

They're giants!' his face red with excitement and his fingers digging into my arm like pincers. However, I understood how he felt. No matter how many whale documentaries you've seen, you can have no inkling of the stupendous bulk of the animal unless it's with you in the water. And here was Henry Jacka face to face with one, a lofty creature with a wise solemn eye, standing on its tail, looking through a glass wall, asking him to listen and understand. That whale might have weighed thirty-six tonnes. And yet the humpback is only a middling whale, small when compared with the fin, the sperm, the peaceful blue, which is more than twice as big as a humpback, and in its great days sometimes reached more than sixty metres in length.

A whale is so large that when it submerges it leaves a dent in the sea's surface. Yet it so radiates tranquillity a human being cannot be afraid of it. This old bull, looking pleasantly at Henry all the while, swept his huge white flipper within a hand's breadth of the glass, careful not to touch or damage. Yet one of this kingly being's favourite games, when in the Antarctic, was to push over icebergs weighing many hundred tonnes.

Loud and urgent I received the message of the whale. So did Stig.

'Well, I'm not surprised,' he said sadly. 'Will you come with me, Riko?'

I was proud that my brother asked for my help. As a seaperson I was a failure in so many ways that I was grateful to be skilled in communication with dolphins and whales. Stig and I must have both sent our agreement to the bull at the same moment, for he shot upwards. The crumpled foil of the surface shattered into blinding sunshine. The roar of his tail cracking through air made our ears pop. He crashed down that

tail twice, three times, and then he was underwater again, plunging away, so powerful, so supple, that I was breathless.

'You come as well, Sif,' said Stig. 'And you, Henry.'

Anyone could see Henry was torn between longing to get out there amongst the whales, and doubt of his swimming ability. He wanted to rush to scramble into his wetsuit, but Stig poured scorn upon him.

Henry looked desperate. 'I must have my breathing gear. I'm not experienced enough without it —'

'Fiddle faddle!' boomed my brother. 'I'm not going anywhere with one of those blasted fizzpots, clucking and bubbling like an old turkey. We'll fit you with a rebreather, my boy.'

'Right you are!' agreed Henry, delighted.

His enthusiasm made the seapeople smile, though they must have been disturbed by the whales' message, which they had caught as clearly as Stig and I had done. Of course Henry knew about rebreathers, which at that time were used by numbers of Navy divers and submarine scientists. But he didn't know how superior our apparatus was. It could safely take a swimmer to twice the depth provided by the Navy unit. And Stig, under his own lungpower, could dive far deeper.

Stig warned Henry to keep close to Sif, to follow her as one dolphin follows another. For although a whale never wishes to hurt a human swimmer, the slipstream of its passing is like that of an express train.

'Don't worry,' I said. 'They'll see in an instant that you're a new person around here. They'll look after you.'

And this was so. By the time we were out in the ocean, warmer now, and full of dancing light, the whales had withdrawn. We saw them through veils of dusky blue —

many, many of them. Their white bellies were like clouds in that blue.

Only the elderly bull, an auntish female and a young bull waited for us. The young fellow was unused to humans. His eye, blue-black as a piece of quartz, looked us over with a half-shy, half-thrilled expression. I supposed that the old father had brought him along to learn that humans in the water are toothless, clumsy little bits of nothing much. Only in ships or even small boats could they be dangerous to him, and should then be watched from a distance.

I sent out those waves of love that always get from a dog an excited waggle of the hindquarters. And, sure enough, the young fellow's tail flukes rippled all along their length. Embarrassed, he whisked away after the elder whales, and I followed. On another day I might have flirted around with him, made him a friend, but my heart was too heavy for that.

The whales' message had been that the lovely waters of the Epiphanies were no longer safe for them; they would never come back to Rongo again.

For hundreds of thousands of years the clans of the southern hemisphere humpbacks had travelled the same ocean roads from the Antarctic's summer seas to the warm winter waters between the Equator and Capricorn. In their sociable way, several clans would set out together, wheeling placidly along through the foggy islands south of New Zealand, then dividing into three or four streams around those enchanting green isles. They took their time on that tremendous journey, playing and chatting, the cows growing heavier with young, the old fathers keeping an eye on everyone. At last they reached their various destinations, the Cook group, or the New Hebrides, or the myriad Fijis.

But now that had to change. The whales had conferred and decided to follow another sea road, far out through the landless waste of water south of Easter Island. There the ocean floor is crazed with fracture cracks. No islands grow in that desert. They do not reappear until the voyager is near the west verge of the Peru-Chile Trench, an abyss that follows the continental coast from Middle America to beyond Cape Horn. Even Kopu lies in more hospitable waters than those.

Their numbers grew smaller season by season, said the whales. Conservationists did not seem to be able to prevent poachers and pirates from preying upon them. Oil slicks were a deadly trap.

Also, the ocean was no longer a lifegiver. The sweetfields, the sandy stretches where springs of freshwater tickled their way up from the bottom, gladly used by the whales to rid themselves of lice and barnacles, now belched out suffocating clouds of mud. They would show Stig these things.

I was glad when the young whale waited for me to catch up, giving me sideways glances of daring and mischief. I took hold of his dorsal fin and lay along his side close to the spine. It seemed to me he took off like a submarine, but he was swimming slowly and carefully, so as not to hurt or frighten his passenger, the little bit of nothing much.

Chapter 7

We swam far beyond the kelp forest. Henry rested
frequently. Even with the rebreather he quickly
tired. Sif lingered with him. And I grew more and more
frightened, of what I did not know.

At last the bull whale halted, upright, flippers across
his belly. If he were not praying, I was. The seafloor
showed a hideous gash that snaked away to the north. It
was so wide you could have dropped into it one of those
monstrous ocean liners of the past. The chasm had the
look of a fatal wound, and like a fatal wound it dribbled
dark, sticky fluid, so hot it stung my skin. I noticed the
whales took care not to swim through the water it
discoloured.

Stig and I shot up to the surface. His ruddy face was
full of dismay.

'That fissure has been there for ever,' he said. 'But
only two weeks ago I could have jumped it. And just
look there, Riko!'

Half a kilometre away, the ocean swelled into inex-
plicable turbulence, rumbling like a boiling pot, loosing
gas bubbles that wobbled for a second and burst. The
stench was suffocating.

When we returned to the depths, the whales led us
further westward, to a place of currents. Hundreds of
reefs and shoals shaped these streams, coiled and looped
them, and let them run. Rivers of brackish water curved

around invisible banks or lay in uncharted ponds as though another world of shapes and boundaries existed unseen. From the beginning of time these warmer, fresher flows were used as highways by all the sea beasts.

But now they were deadly streams. They churned with death — rotten vegetation, harbour debris, a half-eaten crocodile, a swollen grouper, all head and gape. Also there was another dead thing with nightmare head and a ropey body twenty metres long. Henry looked at it aghast.

Stig swam to the herdmaster and put his face against the whale's enormous brow. I did the same to the nervous youngster, but all I could sense was fear.

'What does it all mean?' he asked, in his own way. And I asked it, too.

By the time we arrived back at the city we were exhausted, too fatigued to speak. Stig dried his head and beard, muttering to himself. He put his arm around me.

'You understand, Riko,' he said at last.

I nodded, not daring to speak, because I knew I would begin to sob and disgrace myself. He relied on me, you see, to be strong and sensible, not to give in to my sorrow. He knew the situation was urgent, that everyone in the city was in danger. I swallowed hard.

'The whales are right to go,' I said at last. 'And so are you.'

He left us then, staring exhaustedly at one another.

'I don't think I can bear it,' muttered Henry. He might have meant the gruelling swim, the desperate fatigue. But I understood he meant the knowledge that was now his. The crack that was like an opening into hell. The current that was a travelling graveyard, poisoning far reefs and atolls.

'Damn all landcrabs!' said Henry, putting his head in his hands.

'You can't blame people like us, Henry,' I tried to comfort him.

'I'm a landcrab,' said Henry, 'and I'm ashamed of my own kind. But I don't know what to do about it, that's what I can't bear.'

Sif began suddenly to cry. I'd quite forgotten her. She was cold and pale, and I could hear her teeth rattle. I became very anxious.

'We swam too far,' I said. 'You've got chilled.'

'It's been a bad day for us all,' said Sif. 'You too, Riko. And Henry, such a shock to see a sea serpent —'

She even tried to smile, but the tears ran just the same. We wrapped her up warmly but still her teeth chattered. Stig sent a message to the Island boy to bring the runabout close to the city. Though he loved Sif so much, I could tell his mind was on his other urgent responsibilities.

'She's just being Sif,' he told Henry. 'Things get too much for her.'

It was such a bright, bright day that for half a minute I had to keep my eyes squeezed tight. Squatting there on the wet boards I soon became warm. The sea hissed past, the sky glistened. Even the air seemed to have a polish on it. For a few moments I began to feel I might survive after all, even if I never saw my mother or my brother again. But not without Sif. I needed her. I needed to look after her as I always had. Surely she must feel the same? Worry enveloped me like a shower of rain. Dockie believed that she might choose to go.

'Oh, what does he know about girls?' I thought contemptuously.

On this visit home Dockie had given me too many jolts. He had let me down. I realised that I would have to keep a close eye on anything he decided for Sif and me.

'Just imagine Sif going to a freezing, lonely place like Kopu!' I told myself indignantly. 'She has to be helped to make up her mind the right way.'

It was plain to me that it was my duty to help, though I didn't know how I would do that. However, ideas would come. They always did.

As usual, when I made a decision, I felt more cheerful. I liked small boats, and began to enjoy this one. I whuffled up the air that rushed past. The air in the undersea city had been fresh, but this had a different freshness. Trees had been at work on it; the earth had sucked it down to the plant rootlets and let it trickle out again, damp and delicious. The rain had washed it over and over again. But there was some taint on the wind that day, coming and going, leaving a taste of tarnished brass on the tongue. I knew that odour. It was the breath of the volcano.

As we approached the Island, the boat swooshed high in the air, and a big wave crawled swiftly up the beach to the foot of the coconut groves.

'Whoo!' bawled the Island boy. 'That some good shake, eh, Riko?'

In the boat Henry had sat with his arm around Sif, her head on his shoulder, his big hand holding both hers. He had looked down at her with such an expression. It made me feel lonesome, and the Islander romantic.

'Give us a kiss, Riko, baby!'

'Never mind your kisses, you just watch what you're doing, you great lump!' I yelled, as he crashed the boat into the jetty steps.

He was a good boy, though. While Henry tied up the

139

motorboat, he lifted Sif like a feather and carried her to the bungalow.

Mummy Ti put Sif to bed, scolding her lovingly as she did so.

'Always you do things too hard,' she said. 'Little girl, you want to climb mountain. Big girl, you want to hug whole world. But your arms not long enough, darlen.'

Though Dockie practised very rarely he was still a doctor. He had an oldfashioned stethoscope, a queer thing, but I suppose it did its work well enough. I left him examining Sif's chest, and went out to the kitchen. Mummy Ti was making tea, praying loudly as she did so, whether to Mr Spry's deity or her tribal gods I did not know. I took the teapot away, and gave her a good hug.

'What really the matter with Sif, darlen?'

'She got overtired, and chilled to the bone.'

She shook her head. 'What truly matter, Rikoriko?'

'Matira says Sif must go with her to Kopu,' I said baldly. Mummy Ti's expression changed; the big brown flower of a face became taut; the eyes bulged ferociously; her lips drew back and showed teeth white and sharp as a dog's.

'That Matira! Selfish woman! If she do anything to hurt you or my Sif I put bad words on her.'

'Hey,' I said. 'You a witch?'

'No witch,' growled Mummy Ti. 'I holy Christian woman. All the same, I know a few things. You tell me, Riko. What she say?'

She glowered as I described how our mother had coaxed and then commanded Sif to make ready for the long voyage. She said nothing at the end, but looked at me so seriously that I took fright.

'She couldn't *make* Sif go, could she?'

'Sif pulled two ways, poor girl. Your brother and Matira on one hand, you and Henry on the other. Still, she must make up her own mind, Riko. You keep out of it.'

She sighed and went off with the tea tray. Soon Henry knocked, and came into the kitchen with our belongings from the boat. He asked about Sif and I reassured him.

'See you for supper, Henry?'

He shook his head. 'What with one thing and another, I'm bushed. And I've got more things to think about than I can start counting. I plan to write up some notes and then turn in.'

He did a funny thing then. He leaned over and kissed me on the cheek.

'You're a good brat, Riko.' He put his fist alongside my chin, grinned, and went off. I had no idea what all that meant, but I was amazed and pleased. He kissed differently from Pig, whose kisses were like damp explosions. I promised myself I'd think about that later.

I might even have told Mummy Ti about it when she returned, but she looked upset. She blew her nose with the sound of a conch trumpet. 'That little Sif, so pale. Worn out she is.'

'It was a hell of a swim,' I said. 'And don't forget I did it, too.'

'Oh, you,' she scoffed. 'Sif not like you, darlen. Not tough like old boot.'

Deeply offended, I stamped away to shower off the salt. Who wants to be an old boot? I knew I was sensitive, brimming with good qualities, but no one except Pig seemed to recognise those qualities. I had a great longing to see him.

141

It was blissful under the shower. Naturally I still had problems, and I was fed to the back teeth with them. But I was tired, and so was my brain. I'd cope with the problems tomorrow. As I slowly dried myself, the volcano grunted, a solemn sound in the deep Island darkness — hah-hah-hah high in the air, just letting us know it was there. All the tropical fish rushed into one corner of the tank, a spangled heap of fins and tails. Dockie's shaving brush bounded off the shelf above the basin, and I thought vaguely that we seemed to be having more tremors than usual.

After supper I fell down on my bed, which Mummy Ti and Dockie had moved out to the verandah so that Sif would not be disturbed. When Dockie came to say goodnight, I had to push open my eyelids with my fingers.

'Dockie, Sif isn't really sick, is she?'

He made that maddening Scots noise that sounds like mm-mphm, but I wasn't falling for that. I pinched my leg to awaken myself properly, and kept at him until he said reluctantly:

'Well, there's not that much of her, is there, lass? Do you know what I mean?'

I did. When we were young, if measles hit the school, I had a few spots and a sniffle, but Sif went to the infirmary, and the nurse put on one of those professional faces. After a tough game of tennis, all I felt was hunger, but Sif was wrung out for hours. It wasn't that she complained about the habit she had of taking things badly. That was just the way it happened to her.

Sif had had many shocks that day. So had I, but then, I was an old boot. Dockie knew very well that if he'd done his duty, Sif would have been saved at least one blow, and I told him that.

'Be that as it may,' he said stiffly, 'I've told her she has to stay in bed for a day or two.'

'But is she all right, Dockie?'

'Mmmm-mphm!' He grunted. 'We'll see, we'll see.' I suppose he knew that I was likely to explode with frustration, because he suddenly gave me this blue twinkle and said: 'Whose side are you on, anyway, Riko?'

I fell into sleep like a rock into a well. Some time before sunrise my eyes snapped open. The idea must have been in my head all night, because my first thought was: 'I see what Dockie means! He thinks the same way as I do — it's the best thing for Sif if she stays behind. So he's fixing it that she does. He's pretending she's ill. Sif will believe him because he's a doctor. And so will Mother.'

In a flash Dockie went back to being the smartest old man in the world. I felt so relieved that I didn't know whether to laugh or cry. Everything was going to be all right.

The next day Sif was content to stay in bed, half asleep. I did a lot of goofing off myself, and Henry stayed in his shack. I snooped through the window once. He was writing in another one of his yellow notebooks and didn't look up. I thought myself unobserved, but he murmured:

'Oh, Riko. That creature. *Was* it a sea serpent?'

I answered as carelessly as he: 'Yes, but they're not snakes, you understand. They're colossal worms. Stig says they burrow in the ooze and only come to the surface when they're being chased.'

'Understandable,' said Henry. I went away, grinning.

Sif coughed and wheezed. Her voice was hoarse. To Mummy Ti's loving questions, she only said: 'Oh, I have a cold or something. It's nothing. I was often like

143

this in Sydney. Have you — have you seen Henry?' she asked.

'He hasn't looked in today, darlen,' answered Mummy Ti. To my surprise Sif seemed panic-stricken.

'He hasn't . . . he hasn't left the Island?'

'Of course not!' I was surprised. 'Why would he do that?'

'I just thought — he might have changed — people do,' said Sif almost to herself.

The day went. I knew I had to think seriously sooner or later, about my mother, about the city. About everything. But I was too restless. I made up my mind to climb the mountain the next day and find out what Pig thought. He was a Stone Age boy, but in many things he was very sensible.

So, the next morning, I jumped out of bed and put my head through the vines to see if it was the kind of day for visiting Pig. Though it was near sunrise, there was still little light — only heavy greyness, coiling and writhing with fog.

This happens every now and then on Rongo, as it does on all islands. A cloud comes down and sits on the land, gathering everything to itself, so that car headlights are cast back by a white steamy wall a metre in front of the bonnet. Roads disappear, the sea is only a rumour, and when the sun eventually rises it is a bluish pearl button in the sky, if you can see it at all.

On Big Island, when this happened, you sometimes heard the tourist plane whining round and round above the cloud, the passengers in brilliant sunshine, but the island just a heap of white feathers. Of course a plane can't land in such weather without a navigational tower down below, and Big Island airport had none. The little plane just had to scutter away back to Tonga and try again another day.

I was grateful to see that fog. Surely Tane must be watching over me. I dressed quickly, and crept in to see if Sif were awake.

'Where are you going, Riko?'

'Just up the mountain. Would you like a hot drink or anything?' I lit the lamp and saw that her face was flushed and her eyes glazy.

'Have you been crying?'

'There's nothing the matter with me,' she said irritably. 'I wish you all would stop fussing.'

'I'm not fussing,' I pointed out. 'Unless a hot drink is a fuss.'

She sighed. 'Poor Riko, I'm sorry. I'm just so bothered about everything. Please don't go up the mountain today. I simply have to see Stig and Mother again and I'll need you to swim with me.'

'Oh, don't be a dope, Sif!' I snapped. 'In the first place Dockie would have a fit if you mentioned doing such a thing, and in the second place you can't, because there's a fog as thick as porridge.'

I pulled aside the curtain and raised the window a little. Mist smoked in, bringing with it a rank salty smell.

'You see?' I asked. 'Now snuggle down and forget about swimming. You couldn't move a step until this lifts. And for goodness sake stop fretting. The family mightn't leave for Kopu for weeks.'

'I can't help fretting,' she burst out. Tears came into her eyes again. 'I don't know what to do. I just feel torn apart.'

All at once I was angry. I glared at her.

'You're not the only one,' I said. 'I can't go to Kopu because of the way I'm made, but that doesn't mean I'm not losing my brother and mother. Maybe things are worse for me than they are for you. You're older, and you have Henry — ' here I was pleased to hear an indignant quaver in my voice. 'What have I got? A menehune, that's what. That's why I want to go up the mountain, to see Pig. He cares what happens to me.'

I didn't add, 'And maybe I'm losing my sister as well,' because I knew she'd think of that.

Now, all I'd said was perfectly true, but as everyone knows, a thing can be true in more than one way. It all depends on the manner in which you say it. I knew that my words would strike Sif to the heart. She hadn't had time to think of me as yet; her own future had looked too uncertain. But I steeled myself. It was all in a good cause, I thought.

The mountain path was wide enough only for one person. The fog ghosted in on both sides; it was like walking a wet plank, suspended in mid-air. Did the precipice fall away on this side or that? The uncanny silence made me nervous. There was no wind, the birds were mute; I could catch no sea sigh from far below. When I came to a rock slab, I pressed my ear against it, relieved to hear the gut sounds of the volcano — the rattle of small rock slides in the crater, the whistle of escaping steam, the constant grumble-umble far down in the earth. That volcano was a kind of pet to us, a good-natured dragon, with a voice that had been familiar since I was born. Those growls meant no more to me than a hunger rumble in a grandfather's stomach.

Higher up the mountain, beyond the lava flows, the

146

mist grew thin and gauzy; there were tunnels and caverns of open air. Tops of trees floated like spectral islets in the whiteness. At last I heard muffled sounds, and with relief I realised I must be near the menehune camp.

But the sounds were of an unexpected kind — thumps and loud grunts, laughter and shouts. I couldn't understand it. Were the little people playing a game? Caution told me to approach quietly. I crouched down beside a mighty boulder and watched. Spied — the very thing menehune hate most of all. And so I saw a battle.

There are many legends of fairy battles, high in the air, events of fierce music, floating banners and glittering helmets. This was not like that. All the younger male menehune, and two or three of the older men, were gathered in the open space amongst the boulders, battering away at each other with clubs. The thumps I had heard were blows on the rock-hard heads, the laughter came from the contestants. The battle was far from a game. One of the warriors tottered from the battlefield with blood streaming from a squashed nose. Another had lost a strip of scalp. He seemed to think it a great joke, and half-blinded by blood, looked around for more heads to whack. It was my friend Pig, good tempered as ever, laughing joyfully, but continuing to hammer his brothers and cousins as if they were enemies. I had never seen anything more comic, the squatty figures floating in and out of the mist like trolls or goblins, seemingly in slow motion, not ducking or evading blows, just giving and taking. The thing was a tournament, I realised, and the last man left standing was the winner.

Little menehune women peeped from burrow entrances or crouched behind stones and bushes, darting out and dragging away the fallen, cooing and clucking.

Soon there were only two combatants left in the clearing, and with Stone Age pride I saw one of them was Pig. The other was my non-friend Mud. I was sure that Mud would try to trick Pig in some way, so I scrabbled around behind me for good-sized pebbles which I could hurl at him if Pig started getting the worst of things. Instead of stones I found a hand, hard as iron.

'What you doing, bad Riko?'

I almost jumped out of my skin.

'Father Axe!' He stood over me, his face harsh. He looked so broad, so inhumanly strong that for the first time I thought how frightening menehune could be if they wished. Frightening and alien.

'I wasn't spying, honestly, Axe,' I quavered. 'I just wanted to visit Pig —'

He seized me by the scruff, and I was whisked into the air and dangled like a kitten. As I was taller than he, my feet bounced and dragged on the ground as the pair of us flew down the slope away from the camp. As we went I heard a bawl from Pig.

'Pig's hurt!' I pleaded. 'I want to see if he's all right. Axe, please!'

He dumped me roughly on the ground. Humiliated, I gasped: 'I wasn't spying. Truly, Father Axe. And you know I've never lied to you.'

'No,' he said reluctantly. 'I believe. But no good for big person to see menehune custom.'

'But Pig . . .?' I really was upset about Pig, the blood and the yell, and the knowledge that Mud was such an unprincipled creep.

'Pig all right. You go home, Riko. Not mix in menehune business.' He seemed to be seeking for the right words, and when they came out I didn't like them. 'You stickybeak, Riko. You bossy. Always want to fix things

148

for other people. You go home, Riko.'

So I did. I didn't want to look any more on his grim face. It was terrible to go away from my old friend without the usual nose-rub, without an affectionate word, but I went. The fog was lifting; I could see the path before me, and sometimes a bright glimpse of ocean or sunlit green. I was wobbly from no breakfast and the fright I'd had, and the disturbing knowledge that, although I was innocent, I had offended Axe. So I was pleased when I heard flying footsteps behind me, and the voice of Pig, calling me to wait.

I explained how I hadn't meant to spy, and had continued to watch the battle scene only because I was afraid he would be hurt. In fact, Pig looked the most frightful mess that ever stood upright on its feet — his hair matted with blood, one eye closed, and a bruise from eyebrow to chin. Still, he was cheerful.

'Mud won. He knock me down and trample on my face, good old Mud. Now he get married.'

I was glad to sit down and hear what he had to say. It seemed that in some other island group (Pig called it by its menehune name, so I could not identify it) a girl had been found. She was twelve years old and her name was Fly. She was offered as a wife to some young man of the Epiphany tribe and, as was their custom, they had all done battle for the honour.

'Here, wait a moment,' I interrupted, 'how did you hear about Fly?'

'Oh, we hear it in the air like always,' said Pig matter-of-factly. 'So you see, Riko, I very nearly married man.'

'I thought you loved *me*,' I said huffily.

'I do, I do, Riko,' he said, smacking a kiss on my ear. 'But you too big, you always say. You stick in burrow like fat rabbit.'

149

'Thanks a lot!' I yelped. Still, I was only teasing, and I wished my friend had been the lucky one and won himself a wife. If I'd been there with my handful of pebbles, Mud wouldn't have come out on top, you may be sure.

'And Father Axe said I was bossy!' I complained, needing comfort.

'Father Axe bang on,' said Pig admiringly. 'Sure you bossy. You bossy like man with gun.' I got a smacker on the other ear. 'I love you all the same!'

I hadn't told Pig a thing about the problem of Sif; I'd been too excited over the battle, and so had he. The more immediate puzzle was the way Father Axe had barked at me. I thought about it most of the way home. Constant earth tremors vibrated the ground under my feet. Doubts shook my mind. How could *I* be considered bossy? Always, old Axe had growled, fixing things for other people. But that was because I saw the right thing to do. There was Sif, for instance. It was Matira who was domineering with Sif. Or was it myself, longing for my sister to stay, and working quietly towards that end? Was I to do nothing, say nothing, and allow a person I loved to make a dreadful mistake?

The mist had lifted. A diamond-clear sky and sea lay before me. Far out in the dancing water I saw a solitary swimmer and wondered. The Islanders, though they can all swim months before they can walk, don't take long swims for fun, any more than a fish would. They prefer to surf, or frolic with their friends.

All swimmers have their own style. In a moment, my heart sinking, I recognised this one as my sister. As soon as the fog lifted, she had slipped out to swim to the city.

Words like Dope! Knucklehead! Reckless idiot! scorched through my mind as I flew down the track. Nothing much else did. I was consumed by a dreadful sense of danger. I had seen through Dockie; I knew Sif was not ill, just strung-out and a bit breathless. But even a person with a plain ordinary cold shouldn't take a long swim. The very fact that Sif was swimming above water showed me she'd found she couldn't hold her breath for long beneath it.

As I raced through the banana grove I saw Mummy Ti on the deserted jetty. She flopped into a dinghy tied beside it. Then I spotted Henry running down the jetty. I yelled at them: 'Wait for me, wait for me!'

By the time I reached them, too winded for speech, Henry had Mummy Ti back on the jetty, and was in the dinghy himself, his hand on the outboard motor starter. I pointed out to sea, where I had last seen Sif, and he nodded. The motor spluttered into life, and we bounced away over the water, leaving Mummy Ti standing along, clutching her chest. Poor Mummy Ti! Finding Sif gone from her bed, she had glimpsed her in the water, and run all the way to the jetty. Mummy Ti was not built for running; she was not built for frights, either. I thought: 'If we manage to save Sif, I'll kill that girl!'

'Where's Dockie?' I yelled at Henry.

'Ti says he went off early to Big Island to arrange an X-ray for Sif. This boat must belong to one of the Islanders.'

His face was grim. He wore only his pyjama pants, for Mummy Ti had roused him from sleep as she ran past his shack. But he had a blanket with which to wrap Sif should we find her. Sensible Henry.

'Why did she go?' he shouted.

'If you'd come around yesterday to see how she was

you'd know,' I replied unfairly. 'She's been nearly out of her mind fretting whether she'll leave with Mother or not.'

He didn't answer. Just then we both saw Sif. She had turned and was swimming back towards the Island, floundering along with that slow flabby stroke of the weary swimmer. Henry cut the motor and we coasted up beside her.

'What's the matter with you, dummo?' I shouted 'You might have drowned.'

'Please shut your big mouth,' said Henry quite gently; he slid over the side to support Sif. Just as well, as it is very difficult to hoist up an exhausted person into a small boat without upsetting it. She huddled in the bottom, retching painfully.

'I took a little water aboard,' she croaked. She tried to smile at us. 'Sorry. Giving trouble.'

'Hush now,' said Henry. 'We know.' He wiped her hair and face with a corner of the blanket and wrapped the rest of it around her.

So we returned home. Fortunately my ears are as good as my eyes, so I was able to hear, above the asthmatic racket of the motor, their conversation. Sif said:

'You didn't come to see me yesterday.'

Henry sighed. 'I stayed away because I didn't want to affect your decision. I thought it was the proper thing to do.'

Neither Sif nor I had thought of that. She said timidly: 'Don't you want me to stay?'

'Oh, Sif,' he said 'you're so young. How do you know your own feelings?'

Sif did not reply, though anyone, let alone a person as smart and sensitive as Henry, could have told her answer from her face. With a wry smile he glanced at me. 'Does she, Riko?'

'More than you realise,' I said.

'No, Dockie, I won't go over to Big Island for an X-ray,' said Sif. She was decisive about it, the way I'd always wanted her to be. I had tried to help her be that way, but it was Henry who had done it.

'I have to see Stig and Mother again. Riko must, too.'

'You're not going to swim to the city again, no matter what!' exploded Dockie.

'Your people can come to the lagoon, surely,' suggested Henry gently. 'Riko can get the dolphins to take a message to them.'

He looked at me and laughed, knowing I was thinking what an astounding thing it was that he, of all people, could suggest something that sounded like fantasy. But Henry was a true scientist. Once a thing was proved to him, he began to make intelligent use of it.

The dolphins, when I called them in, were noisy and agitated.

'The whales have gone, gone, gone! We rode their bow wave for a while; and then we became frightened, for they said they would never come back.'

I told them that was true, and they became more excited than ever, feverishly whirling and plunging, clamouring around me.

'Perhaps we should go too! No, we don't want to! These are our islands, dolphin islands. We love you, Riko. What shall we do?'

All I could say was that they must ask Stig. They took our message and shot away like black rockets.

As the sun set that evening, Stig and Matira came to

the lagoon. I was scared; I didn't know what to expect. Also I had that hollow ache in the heart which everyone gets when she hears the sounds of goodbye in the air. I did hear the sounds of goodbye, as I knew my brother and mother did also. The voyage to the new home was full of danger; it would take these warmblooded Pacific people into a part of the ocean they did not know. Their scouts had reported that the submarine city off Kopu was very ancient and partly ruined. I was afraid for Sif, too. I thought that Matira might persuade her to go.

'I'll speak for you,' said Dockie to my sister. But Henry said:

'No, doctor, that's my business now.'

Dockie was very shaky and upset, knowing that he would not see much more of his friends. His eyes were red, not from schnapps, but secret weeping.

'Ah, the old days, the old days, lass!' he said to me.

Mummy Ti insisted on accompanying us. I watched her dress, in the old style — the flowing flowery dress called a Mother Hubbard, her beautiful black hair down her back, and a crown of orange hibiscus flowers on her head. She was majestic, like a Tahitian princess of ancient days. Her face was fierce. I knew she would fight Matira for Sif, if it came to that. I remembered her words, that she would not allow bad things to happen to us.

Whatever was in her mind — pagan spells or Christian prayers — was powerful. She said nothing, crouched on the sand above high tidemark, her eyes fixed upon Stig and our mother. Just the look of her made me feel uneasy. I was thankful it was not me she disliked.

Sif waded into the shallows and put her arms around our mother.

'I can't come with you, Mother,' she said. I knew she was trembling, expecting rage or scorn, or even worse, long persuasions in that voice no one could resist. Yet she spoke firmly, saying that she loved Henry and had to be with him.

Matira's eyes wandered sadly over us, her gaze resting on each one in turn. I noticed then that she was not the dazzling creature of our last meeting; she looked tired and dull, as though a light had been blown out.

'Yes, you must remain behind, Sif.' Her voice was agitated. I was too surprised to utter a sound.

Matira told us that for two or three days she had had a sense of danger. It surrounded all the seapeople, but was blackest about Sif. She did not know what the danger was; she knew only that a great dread was with her day and night. She shuddered, clutching Sif's hand.

'Our mother fears that the journey will be disastrous,' explained Stig. 'She dreams of darkness, a great wave, death. But we must go to Kopu, we have no choice now. So it is safer for Sif to remain with you and Ti,' he said to Dockie. 'Some day we may all be together again.'

He left with Dockie two of the rebreathers and a little bag of Fredrik's emeralds. He also gave Henry the shell of a mollusc thought to be extinct a million years ago. By these things I knew that my people would soon depart on the great voyage.

Yet he lied about it, saying cheerfully that he and Matira would come to the lagoon the following evening. I gulped, the ache in my chest being too much to bear, and he scolded me, calling me his little fish.

It was easier for Sif to believe she would see them again, and I gave him a hug to thank him for lying. As for me I went to bed early, thinking I could not live until morning, the pain of farewell was so great. Some time

155

after midnight I heard the verandah boards creak under Dockie's step. I joined him where he leaned over the rail, and thought about the things that had happened that day.

Before she swam away after Stig, my mother had kissed me and whispered. 'I love you dearly, Rikoriko. You are like your father. But don't be too much like your father. Let those you love go free.'

I didn't know what she meant. But people learn.

So I stood there with Dockie at the rail, waiting for something to happen. It was moonlight; the sea was patched with dark and brightness. All at once something skidded out of the water beyond the reef. I thought it was a manta ray, but it was a skipper. The sea was dark there; the skipper shone like a silver coin. Then another flipped out, many of them. Away they went, not far above the surface, touching down now and then, like stones in that game called ducks and drakes. They disappeared into the dazzle.

I took Dockie's arm, but he shook me off. He was crying; he cried a lot in the days that followed. I suppose that when you are old and you lose your dear friends, much of your own lifetime goes with them. And soon Dockie would have no one except Mummy Ti.

'He talking to that old bottle,' was what Mummy Ti said whenever I could not find Dockie around the place. Some children came from an outlying atoll; their father had been poisoned eating the mysterious dream-fish. The Polynesians *will* eat it; it gives them a high if they're lucky, and delirium and occasional madness if they're not. Ordinarily Dockie would have commandeered the nearest speedboat and raced to that atoll with his stomach pump in half time flat. But this time Mummy Ti couldn't rouse him. It was Mr Spry who got on the radio and had the Big Island doctor clatter out there in the Epiphanies' one helicopter. But the man had jumped out of a palm tree by then and was dead.

Mummy Ti spent her days halfway between annoyance at Dockie, and romantic happiness. If she could have done so, she would have followed Henry and Sif around, just watching and beaming. If Dockie was drunk on schnapps, she was drunk on love.

'My little Sif!' she murmured. 'My lovely Henry!'

I fished and swam and sometimes talked to Henry. Every day Sif looked more like herself. Still, there was that transparent look, and her hands were thin. When I asked her if she felt well again, she only said, 'Everything's perfect.' And it was. When I was around her and Henry I had that golden feeling again. They were somehow enclosed, and yet open to all the world.

Of course there were things I had to say to Henry. I explained how special Sif was, how easily frightened by noise and cruelty and people yelling at each other, the way she panicked when Joanne shouted at Travis for something — her hands over her ears, her eyes wild.

'Joanne never understood,' I said. 'She thought Sif was stupid. But Sif knows a thousand things the rest of us don't. Sometimes I *suspect* them, but she knows them.'

'I understand,' said Henry. 'She's not quite of this world, our rackety old human world. Well, I won't push her into it, I promise.'

I told him how when Sif walked past a Zoo — how she hated Zoos! — all the animals cried out and threw themselves at the bars and the walls. And how I had sometimes found her sitting in the bush, with birds alighting on her hair and arms.

157

'Poor Joanne!' I said, smiling, and I truly meant that.

'There are some people that are more like — ' I was going to say 'spirits' but when I considered it, it sounded crazy, so I stopped and said briskly: 'I guess I'll hear from Joanne any day now, I mean whether she's forgiven me, whether I can go back to Sydney. The money isn't important any more, because of the emeralds Stig gave Dockie, but I want to be friends with Jo and James again. So,' I said, 'I would like to see the undersea city just once more. Would you, Henry?'

Henry wondered, and I did also, whether the sight of the city would upset Sif. So I asked her.

'No,' she said, 'I want to see it. It will always be a part of my life. I'm a seaperson, I can't change that, and Henry knows it.'

She explained that they had agreed that sometimes she would go back to the sea and her own kind, and that way maybe no irresistible homesickness would come upon her, so that she ran away for ever, like Matira.

'Henry understands me better than our father understood our mother,' she said.

'He's a king,' I said. He was, too.

'I know,' said Sif. 'I think it was for Henry, not for me alone, that Mummy Ti gave Mother the fear that something would happen to me if I went with her on the voyage.'

'Well, I've wondered about that,' I said.

'It doesn't matter,' she said. 'I'd made up my mind, anyway.'

Mummy Ti had been very cocky since she visited the lagoon that evening.

'I give Matira bad dreams,' she boasted. 'Nobody cook up horrible dream like Ti.'

'How? Go on, tell me!' I begged, with ideas of giving Joanne a nightmare now and then. But Mummy Ti shook her head, chuckling. She was so convinced that she had filled our mother with fears and premonitions that I got spooky about the whole thing, and during one of Dockie's sober moments, asked him about it.

'I wouldn't put it past Ti to know a wee bit of magic,' he conceded. 'But it's my belief that Matira dreaded the long voyage, and her dreams followed the fear. The seapeople have often surprised me, the things they know.'

'What things, what things?' But he wouldn't tell me, and I was left with the feeling that I'd often had about my mother, much as I loved her, that she knew things other ordinary people didn't. The myths do say that mermaids often warned sailors of danger from shipwreck.

Dockie was in no condition to be asked if it were all right for Sif to visit the city for the last time. Henry inquired of Mummy Ti.

'I'll get one of the Island boys to take us as far as the city in Dockie's boat,' he suggested. 'He'll wait for us and bring us home again. So it won't be too tiring for Sif and the young'un here.'

Mummy Ti rolled up her eyes. She knew I could out-swim Henry with my feet in a sack.

Spring had come to the Epiphanies, if you can ever say that of tropical islands. The year spins on the trade winds and the rains they bring. Still, there is a little while when the islands seem to taste spring, fruit blossom everywhere, and around the church, where the early homesick missionaries planted European flowers, may-be a snowdrop in a moist shaded place.

There was, too, as we spun away from the jetty, the light of spring, silky and greenish. The water was so still, it was daubed as though with white paint by cloud reflections. I felt such a pang that I must leave Rongo, but then, so must Sif. I knew Henry must soon resume work for the Museum.

That day he was wearing his full Loch Ness monster suit, and I thought that maybe he intended to dive rather deeply around the city, on this his last opportunity.

Sif and I had the rebreathers Stig left us. Henry thought it safest. I didn't. My snorkel would have done me. But it was best for Sif. Dockie's boat was in good order; the outboard motor had been recently checked. We scooted over that glassy water so fast we almost flew. The island dwindled. Above it stood a column of steam dense and white like a pillar of salt.

'You've had a lot of earthquakes lately,' observed Henry to the Islander. 'Do you think the volcano's more active?'

The Islander thought the steam was mostly from Steaming Cliff.

'And sulphur! Pooh!' he exclaimed. 'Rocks all yellow with it. Old mountain restless maybe. But everything all right.'

He was the same boy who had accompanied us before. With Sif and Henry in the bow, I was all too close to him. He snuggled up to me and his big hand stroked my knee.

'You got lovely black hair, Riko. You got lovely soft leg, too.'

'And you've got a big flappy mouth!' I hissed.

I put my hand on the shaft of Pig's knife, which I wore almost all the time, mainly as a tease for Henry, who longed to ask more questions about it but was too polite.

160

'Ho ho,' laughed the Islander, 'Riko got teeth, eh? Stick knife in lover boy?'

'Oh, shut up!' I said.

I was surprised to see his brown face turn ashy. He pointed down into the sea.

'*Te mata*! Why? Never before in daylight!'

He cut the motor, and we all stared into the depths, where something like an illuminated coral reef beamed and twinkled.

'Never *te mata* show in daylight!'

He made the sign of the Cross with one hand and with the other clutched a little bag of something pagan that hung around his neck.

Sif glanced around, getting her bearings. 'Why, we're above the city! That's what it is, Riko. They must have left the lights on.'

'Wow!' exclaimed Henry, thrilled. He jammed in his mouthpiece and tipped backwards out of the boat without another word.

As we three plunged downwards through the blue invisibility, towards that wall that sparkled like sequins, sending long diamond-bright rays into the further blue, I thought that as the seapeople had left before dawn, they had wanted a last sight of their home. Sooner or later the stored *te mata* would dim and die; the city would be dark forever. But they had seen it radiant, alive. That would be their memory of it.

The light brought life to the red, orange and yellow that are absorbed by water. The sea around us was a gorgeous garden of fish, freckled and striped, a squid banded in chocolate, a beautiful pale-spotted orange octopus delving amongst the bright green sea-lettuce near the airlock.

In this enchanted world we went wild, flitting about

161

the city, peering through the windows facing the great chasm, chasing each other around the towers like birds. Even Henry, now weightless, was graceful, a huge fantastic raven. He caught Sif by the hair, and they swooped off into the dusky depths. I hung in the water, knowing myself one with the crimson sea slug on the bottom far below, and the big-eyed turtle that paddled past, using its patchwork flippers like slow wings. If a person could sing with purest happiness underwater, I would have done so. I was singing anyway, inside my head.

Other things had been going on all morning inside my head — dolphins chattering, chirping, calling. Somewhere they were racing and frolicking, telling each other hat a fine day it was.

Suddenly there was a piercing cry of alarm, a dolphin cry. Had I heard it with ears or brain? I saw Sif come upright; she had heard it too. The next moment every fish in sight vanished, like a tumult of frightened parrots.

Sound travels well in water. What I heard was a stupendous roar, rumbling, grinding, that almost burst my eardrums. I could not cover my ears; both hands were holding the rebreather. The pain was fearful. I didn't know what had happened; I believed some disaster had happened inside *me*. Then what I thought was smoke puffed out into the water from the reef, the city itself. It was not smoke, of course, but earth and rock. Then the whole city, it seemed, took a step forward, hung in the water an instant and crumbled slowly down upon its own foundations.

The displacement of water hurled me headlong. I clung to the rebreather for dear life, tossing and turning like a chip amongst clouds of debris, big and little, that continued to rush violently from the devastated flank of the Island.

162

Above us, we learned later, the boat was flung several metres into the air, tossing out the Islander and frightening him witless. But fortunately it didn't sink, and he chased it and held on to the stern.

Many times I heard him describe in his own tongue what he saw: 'The water went round and round. There were troughs deeper than trees or houses, even those big houses in cities. And there were waterspouts, too, roaring like thunder, and broken things shooting into the air like rockets, doors and furniture and smashed machinery. I thought it was the end of the world.'

What had happened was that the volcano, threatening for so long, had filled those ancient gas tunnels with mud and steam, the pressure built up, and at last the reef and the city set into it just blew out into the sea, in a colossal landslide.

The strange thing was that for a few minutes the lights continued to burn in part of the ruined city. If not, would we have been able to save Henry? Something heavy had knocked him from behind as he fled, tearing away his air tank, and pinning him to the seafloor. At first I could not see Sif, but as I dived downwards, dodging the swirling, sinking debris, she swooped towards us both, waving me away.

Henry still gripped his mouthpiece, though it was attached to nothing. He was dazed and bewildered. Sif tugged out the mouthpiece, and whipped her own rebreather over his face. His hands were free, and she slapped them on the device. Then she pointed to herself, made the up sign, and was away towards the surface.

I read her signal this way: I was to stay with Henry. She had gone to fetch the Islander for help in freeing him. The Islander was a powerful swimmer; Sif had made a good decision.

163

Henry was not hurt, but his desperate eyes shone through the mask, asking questions, trying to be calm. Giving him a reassuring sign, I scrabbled as best I could around the thing that pinned him down. It was part of a door, inlaid with metal. As far as I could see, it had torn away his air tank completely, and one sharp corner had hammered into the ooze what was left of the harness. The lights in the city were now all gone; the dusky blue had re-established itself, and it seemed to me that the water had become cold. I thought I could see terror in his eyes; his chest heaved irregularly. He was beginning to gulp air, as panicky people do.

I tried to undo the buckles of the harness, or slip it off over his shoulders, but his position defeated me. I pulled out Pig's knife, showed it to Henry to reassure him, and began to saw away at the harness, holding my rebreather precariously in my teeth. Every moment I expected Sif and the Island boy to arrive beside us. Looking up, I saw the boy swimming amongst the debris, searching for us. Just as the knife chewed through the last strap, he saw us, and was able to help Henry to the surface.

But Sif was not there. Sif was not anywhere. I don't know what happened. Probably she had not taken a deep enough breath before she gave the rebreather to Henry. A person can drown very quickly, very easily, even a seaperson if her lungs have been ruined by city life. I dived again and again; so did the Island boy. Once I thought I saw her body floating amongst the flotsam that was beginning to sink in the great chasm — a rag doll, with shifting hair, like seaweed. But I might have been mistaken.

Mummy Ti blamed herself. If she hadn't interfered, if only Sif had gone away with the seapeople! Dockie did

his best to persuade her that nothing she had done had caused Sif's death; it had been the volcano and the destruction of the city.

But she was never sure. And neither was I, in spite of what Dockie had said.

Mummy Ti staggered out to the lawn and sat there in the dew, uttering long howls like a lonely dog. After a while she crawled to a bush, and pulled off green fronds to plait herself the garland of mourning. But I couldn't go to her; I couldn't do anything.

I didn't want to sleep in the room we had shared. I didn't want to see the blue cotton dress thrown over a chair, or the mirror that had reflected the face I loved best in the world. I went out to the camp bed on the verandah. Everything made noises, the shutters rattling, the geckoes cluck-clicking in the rafters, my heart. Noises I could no longer bear. I put the pillow over my head.

Some time in the night I felt Pig's hard hand on my hair. When I sat up, he put his arm around me, not saying anything. We stayed like that until I fell asleep, and then, I suppose, he vanished into the starlight in the way menehune have.

Chapter 8

I t's a long time since this happened. When you think that I was born in 1986, and these things took place in 2000, you can see that I've been grown-up for ages. Sometimes I wonder if I've become as pigheaded as I used to think all adults were. Martin says not, but as he's always on my side of things, that doesn't count. Martin Jacka, I mean, the frog boy.

After Sif died, it was as if the sun didn't rise over Rongo for weeks. Dockie simply faded. He became a withered little jockey of a man, always blaming himself for not telling other people that Sif was in such frail health. He knew her chest was affected. He didn't tell Mummy Ti because he believed she'd worry; he didn't tell me because he thought me too young.

'If only I hadn't been drunk that day you went to the city,' he said over and over again. 'I would have warned Henry she wasn't strong enough.'

Henry was so good with him and Mummy Ti, more like a son than a friend. During the days that I felt my very life had been taken away from me he was kinder than I knew anyone could be. But time went by, and he had to leave for home. We sat in the vine-covered shed that was the Big Island airport, and he told me how he had felt about Sif. Everything.

'For me,' he said, 'it's been like living in another world. Or a legend. I know it's changed many things

166

about me. Not only the way I think, but the way I am, and the way I'll be.' He took my hand. 'Riko, will you write to me sometimes? Because I'm scared that Rongo and what happened here might turn into a dream.'

'Sif, too?' I asked sadly.

'Never Sif.'

There was a call to board, Epiphany style: 'Come on, darlens, what you hanging about for? We sick of waiting!'

Henry laughed. I walked with him to the boarding gate. He said: 'Who really owned that queer old knife, Riko? The one that saved my life?'

'A friend, a menehune.'

'I thought as much,' said Henry. He kissed my forehead and strode away, and I thought, 'Oh, if only there's another like you, somewhere, and around in ten years time!'

A little while later I returned to Sydney. Joanne and James took me back, and I began to work very hard. Joanne told me that the way Sif and I had stuck together over everything, shutting her out, having secrets, had hurt her very much.

'Because I am your sister, Riko,' she said. 'Just as much as Sif was.'

Joanne's calling me Riko instead of Erika made me want to bawl. I had to wait until I was in the shower that night. All the stiff places in my throat and chest seemed to dissolve, partly because I was crying, but mostly because I knew Joanne was sharing the grief with me. Things were better after that.

Not long afterwards a letter arrived from the United States, not from Henry but from Martin Jacka.

'Hi!' it began. 'I'm a frog man. How come you love sea worms?'

167

So, I had to tell him. We wrote to each other on and off for several years. During this time his brother Henry Jacka was building up the fame and respect he later gained, though not in shell-collecting.

For the world didn't end with a bang or anything dramatic and noisy.

A little way into the twenty-first century, as though it were tired of the long battle against mankind, the earth began quietly to die. Like a baby will when you have no real love for it. Rain patterns became wild. That was something to do with the damage to the upper atmosphere. After that came drought and its grey brother famine. Everyone who is young today will remember those times.

During those years many kinds of familiar creatures vanished forever. One day my niece Giselle said wonderingly: 'Do you *really* remember butterflies, Erika?'

In the Pacific all the bordering countries endured the megastorms. They spat out tornadoes and filled the dark skies with upside-down trees of lightning. The rain was like that in the biblical Flood — continental coasts collapsed, mountains fell in, many islands and atolls were stripped right down to their coral bones.

The air shook with the grumbling of volcanoes, even in places like Antarctica and China — unexpected places. There were no vast eruptions, only sinking land, tidal waves, and this shuddering, complaining sound, coming from nowhere and everywhere. The Rongo volcano, however, blew out sideways, blasting away the Steaming Cliff and drowning the leeside of the Island in mud. It was not much of an eruption as eruptions go. No one was killed. Some of the menehune were trapped in their burrows, but safely dug their way out, bad-tempered and hungry. Amongst them was Fly, Mud's young wife, and her two children, especially precious because they were girls. All the big people were evacuated to Big Island. In time they returned home to rebuild their houses and replant their gardens. Not Dockie, though. He had a heart attack and died on Big Island.

'He went off like a lamb,' sobbed Mummy Ti. 'He a gentleman always, my Dockie.'

I thought, yes, he was, and very grateful I am that he gave me my early education. I remembered the last time I saw him was when I was sixteen. He looked like a man made of white paper. We sat out on the verandah and watched the mantas jumping, and I expect we both thought of the same thing. Dockie was pretending to drink schnapps, and I was gloomy. I had seen some terrifying changes in Australia — rivers silted up, the deserts crawling like live creatures towards the green coasts, the disappearance of bees, and the tragedy this meant for all crops.

'Does it have to be this way, Dockie?' I asked in despair.

Dockie had become very gentle, with a feather-thin voice. So I nearly jumped out of my skin when he banged down the glass, and yelled, quite in his old way.

'Inevitable that the world is ruined, is that what you're getting at?'

I murmured something about modern technology.

'It's not modern technology at fault,' he snapped, 'it's the idea you have of it, that it must ruin and destroy. For a long time now, people have had that idea. And they think, poor boobies, that it's the only one.'

He flushed with excitement. 'And if enough people have the same idea, good or bad, my lass, then it will be so. Look at some of the bad ones that have ruled the human mind. Human sacrifice! In its time thought essential for the good of the tribe.'

I saw what he meant. 'Slavery is another idea like that,' I said. 'And religious wars. Child labour. They all look raving mad to us, but they didn't in their own time. Hold on a moment, Dockie. What's *our* lunatic idea?'

'Oh, lass,' he groaned, 'my generation, and yours too, are crawling with crazy ideas. We fell for them like people with hay in their heads. For one: to be happy, you must possess many things. Or many people.'

'Or much power,' I added.

'And to get riches, or possessions, or power you have to destroy, ruthlessly. You *must* get what you want, regardless. And if destruction is the end result, that's inevitable. A woeful shame, of course. Poison the sea so you can take the minerals out of it, cut down forests that took centuries to grow, and let the streams dry up and the land erode into desert, oh, such a pity, but it's inevitable.'

'But Dockie,' I said, remembering an idea I'd had myself when I was young, 'those people who are wrecking our world won't live for ever. We have to find others to take their place, people with good ideas.'

'Or no ideas at all,' said Dockie.

'No one has *no* ideas,' I puzzled, 'except a baby.'

My squawk had brought Mummy Ti pounding out to the verandah. When she saw that nothing bad had happened, she stood in the doorway, listening.

'Babies grow into children!' I exclaimed. 'And children into adults. If people with babies are careful enough, we'll soon have a whole generation of adults who have wonderful, marvellous ideas!'

'And the more people who have those ideas, don't forget, lass, the more there will be who take hold of them. But the first and most important is that ecology isn't something on the outside of us, it's *us*.'

170

Mummy Ti took him by the shoulder. 'Over-excited again!' she said. 'Eyes glittery like dog in the jimjams! Bed for you, old man, or I stamp you flatter than you are now.'

She pulled him away; all the way up the passage I could hear him insisting: 'There's nothing more powerful than the idea whose time has come, you hear me, lass? Go after it, Riko! You and all the others who remember the earth as it once was.'

I contacted Henry immediately about the idea whose time had come.

'Get to it, Henry!' I said.

Grinning, I watched him on the screen. He hadn't changed much; still the same pleasant Henry. Over all those thousands of kilometres his groan nearly blasted off my ear. He gave me a familiar look of exasperation, said I was like a prickle in the toe, and clicked off. Instantly I contacted him again. He said: 'Yes, Riko?'

'Henry,' I said urgently 'The little children have to be brought up the way young dolphins are.'

'Well, of course,' he agreed. 'Goodbye, Riko.'

It was Henry's first book that made people understand that nothing is inevitable, that when many people think the same constructive things they have power over the future. After all it was only in the 1980s that biologists observed that rats, put through certain tests, made a predictable percentage of failures, but that their descendants made fewer failures. And after that rats in another country, put through the same tests for the first time, made few or no failures. It was as though the first successful rats, now in possession of the idea that they could conquer the tests, had in some way dispersed that knowledge to all ratdom.

171

Other enthusiasts founded the educational pro-
grammes for infants and tiny children, but Henry joined
them and made the teaching of planetary support his
lifetime work. As we all know nowadays little children
and babies really are like young dolphins. They're good
and loving and happy. That's if they're left to grow their
own way. They don't want to own a lot of things; they
truly like other beings' company and affection more
than possessions. They're born knowing that the planet
loves them as they love it. Of course children always
were born knowing that. It was just that in the past
people stuffed their heads with greedy ideas, so that they
forgot their own good sense and grew up seeing life the
wrong way.

But you know all this, because, like me, and Martin
Jacka, you belong to the generation that woke up.

Never again did I hear from Stig or any of the sea family,
so perhaps they had never learned about Sif. I was not
surprised that I did not hear. But I never stopped hoping
that one day we might meet again.

During a long vacation, when I was about twenty
years old, I travelled to Kopu, flying to Easter Island and
taking a small store vessel from there. By that time, as
everyone knows, the famous Easter Island statues had
mostly been eaten away to stumps by polluted rain, and
the tourist industry was dead.

'Don't waste your time going to Kopu,' advised the
receptionist at the deserted hotel. 'There's not one thing
there.'

And there was not. Kopu was the peak of a submarine
mountain rising from one of the stupendous deeps of the
Pacific. Its people spoke Polynesian mixed with rough

Spanish, for the island was an almost forgotten possession of Chile. In bygone centuries it had been a simple place, its people getting along happily on fish and pork, and corn and vegetables grown in the stony fields. Now it was wretchedly deserted. Even the jetty had tumbled down, so that I had to be swung inshore on the freight winch.

There was nowhere to lodge. At last I got a bed in the shanty of a suspicious woman with a swollen neck.

'What you want, what you want?' she kept asking. I told her my people had come to Kopu six or seven years before, and she answered flatly that no one had come. The island was dead; there were not enough people left to work the fields. The north-west wind was laden with radiated dust. It had tainted the water table, and now their own wells poisoned them. The chickens and pigs had died long before. Everyone had goitre and sores that would not heal. There was no fresh food. The visiting doctor had told them that canned stuff from Easter Island was safer.

I got nothing out of her, or anyone else on Kopu. I might have gone away believing that my seapeople had perished on the way east. But one day I halted to take a hologram of a tumbledown hut. Before it crouched an old granddad carving a mermaid.

'Souvenir?' he croaked. 'Souvenir of Kopu?'

I browbeat the poor old man until tears ran down his wrinkles. He said that if he talked, his daughter would be furious and not give him his tobacco that week. But I beat him down at last, and he trembled out some questions: Did I want to know about ancient times when the sea tribe lived near the shore of Kopu? Because that belonged to a thousand generations before, when the gods lived in the hills, and the island was warm and

173

fertile. I remembered Stig's telling me that Kopu had been chosen partly because there was an abandoned city there.

'No, no,' I said. 'The other ones who came not so many years ago.'

At last he mumbled that my seapeople had indeed come to Kopu. The Islanders were sworn to silence because it was not good to speak to strangers about those who live beneath the sea. My family, he said, had remained less than a year, and then gone away in their round ships. He didn't know where.

I sent off a boiling letter to Henry Jacka about these poor Islanders, their swollen necks, their exhausted look, the way their children died young. I wrote to Martin, too.

'Why are you wasting your time with frogs?' I demanded. 'Your place is with Henry.'

I returned to Easter Island, feeling as though I had come to the end of my search, and that I would never hear anything of my family again. The island is a lonesome place. The wind whines in the long grass, where faces of abandoned statues look up indifferently, telling nothing about their meaning, why they were sculpted, what were their names. They are deeply pitted by the caustic rain; as I patted a long haughty nose the stone crumbled to grit under my hand. I gave myself up to gloom. What hope was there for anything?

After a while I noticed a man walking towards me, his sandy hair blowing around in that tetchy sea wind. A young man, no older than myself, in a thin bright shirt. As he came closer I saw that he looked like Henry Jacka, except for the glasses.

'Martin?' I asked unbelievingly.

'Your letter made me feel it was time we met,' he said. 'I'm cold. Give me a piece of your coat.'

Inside me a voice said: 'Your turn one of these days, ol' Riko!'

And so it was. We sat there beside the derelict giant, my parka spread across both our shoulders against the knifing wind, and talked our heads off.

'You're right about the frogs,' he admitted. 'They're pretty fair at looking after themselves. But I won't join Henry. He has a good part of the world on his side already.'

He told me then that he was joining me, if I and my colleagues would have him, to devote his life to the rescue and rebreeding of almost extinct sea mammals.

This became almost a family affair, Joanne's children Giselle and Travis joining the team when they were old enough. Both of them turned out to be seapeople. Joanne let them lead their own lives without making things hard for them. There was more merwoman in her than any of us had thought.

Although Martin and I have been so happy together, there is always that part of me that hankers to know what became of the seapeople. Every time I see an island half lost in sun-dazzle, its lagoon shimmering green and blue like abalone shell, I think of Rongo where I was born, where Matira was born. Where is she, my mother? Only once did I find myself on the threshold of finding out.

I was taking temperature readings of one of east Australia's inshore currents, when a bull whale surfaced near my boat. He came up with care, but the rubber dinghy bounced like a ball. He rolled a little so that one eye could look me over. His head was so infested with barnacles it seemed as if it were studded with huge nails.

'Poor old battler!' I thought, knowing the pain and irritation these parasites cause. Instantly a picture filled my mind — this same whale breaching and diving under

175

a waterfall that smashed down from melting ice cliffs. I knew this is how whales rid their hides of pests — in cold fresh water. The whale was answering civilly that soon he too, would find ease and comfort.

For a moment the queerness of this did not strike me. When it did, I was very excited. I had not been able to communicate with sea animals since I was fifteen, for such communication is a faculty that belongs mostly only to children. I was so delighted I could scarcely calm down enough to ask his age and tribe. He answered that he had known twenty breeding seasons and was of the elder Fijian family.

'I had a family once,' I thought. Immediately, another picture came to me; Stig and my mother, not much changed, though there was white in his beard and in her hair.

'Have you news of them, old father?' I asked eagerly. 'What happened to them after they left Kopu?'

My mind was so out of practice the pictures the whale gave me were muddled and half-formed. It was like viewing a film run through in a hurry — a muddy boiling sea, a grey island I recognised as windswept Kopu. Then another with a crimson sky and howling volcano, terrifying! But before I could cry out, the whale showed me an immense white wall. I knew it at once. It was the Ice Barrier, the fence of the South Pole.

'Did they go there? But how could they live in those waters?'

That glittering wall dissolved, and before my mind's eye appeared a marvellous island, so high and pinnacled it was swept by showery clouds full of rainbows. It was like one of those islands dreamed of by seventeenth-century explorers — a raft of palms and flowery trees, floating amidst aquamarine lagoons.

'But where is it? What is its name?'

'It is Meru.'

As with the dolphins, I did not know whether this name came to me as a word. I know only that it murmured through my mind, a certainty impossible to describe. Far away I saw the spouts of the bull's impatient family, all blowing north as the herd wheeled majestically towards Antarctica. In a moment he was gone. My boat was almost swamped in the flurry of his tail.

'Where is it, where is it?' I shouted with much of my old power of mind. But distantly there came to me only the thought: 'Meru! Meru!'

My work has taken me to every sea and ocean, but I have never found Meru. How can such an island remain undiscovered? Perhaps, I have sometimes fancied, it is like one of the islands in the legends, able by enchantment to hide themselves in mist and mirage.

But Martin reminds me that in India — the Irihia which was a stopping place for the Polynesian tribes on their long journey towards the east — there is a tradition that somewhere stands a very high mountain, the home of the god Vishnu, marking the middle of the world. It is called Meru.

I don't know what this means; I don't even know what I want it to mean. Sometimes when I am lonely or sad I feel it must mean that my seapeople are all dead now, and that the mysterious name Meru belongs to an otherworld place, a kind of Paradise. To my family, Paradise would always take the form of a delicious island in the Pacific.

But the sea tribes are not all gone. Now and then a dolphin or whale manages to get a message into my head, though it is often too garbled to feel sure about. There is a small colony off Sumatra in the East Indies, and Canada has an underwater city amongst the Queen Charlotte Islands on the Pacific coast. A sperm whale told me that there are a few cold-resistant old things holed up in a submarine cave system on the tail-end of South America. Then there is a thriving city under the largest of the Scilly Isles, south of England. It has a romantic history, for it was founded in the days of King Arthur; the great enchanter Merlin, it is said, laid out its streets and courts. But that city fell upon hard times, and only in the last twenty years have refugee seapeople gathered there, to become a community once more. Yes, there are a few of our kind left, after all. But it seems to me that as yet no one leads the same kind of free life that Sif and I did when we were children. Except perhaps the menehune.

Not long ago Martin and I visited Rongo, which he had never seen. The Epiphanies came out of the heat haze in the way they do — the folded valleys full of cloud shadows, the lofty peaks lost in the clouds themselves. It is only when the aircraft is close that you see the hideous wounds of strip-mining on Big Island, where in years past the developers tore off the forest as a hunter might rip the hide from an animal. And the lee side of Rongo is a moonscape of paint-red mud, solidified into crumbling rock.

Close by the new pre-fab village stands Mr Spry's roofless church, its nave crowded with treeferns and palms. There is a new chapel near the mission house, which was not touched by the eruption. I noticed that the stone bathroom was still in use. Our old bungalow and the general store collapsed and burned in the disaster, but there's a little supermarket in their place, stocking the same old junk foods the Rong'ans love.

It was the same, and yet not at all the same. No Mummy Ti welcomed me with wide-open arms and cries

178

of joy. Soon after Dockie's death, she returned to her own little island, and there she lives peacefully. Martin and I saw her on the same trip, and I asked if she were happy.

'Don't worry, darlen,' she said. 'Life it turn and turn, and us with it, like a big wheel.'

She enfolded Martin's lanky form in her vast arms.

'You a good boy,' she said, 'but not like my lovely Henry.' She sighed. 'This ratty little girl here, this Riko, she not too bad. But ah, you should have seen her sister Sif.'

'I think I have,' said Martin. 'I think I do.'

Of course I wanted to visit the menehune, for I longed to see Pig again. It was scorchingly hot toiling up those dark lava fields, and across the slipping, rattling falls of scoria. Martin took my hand. I knew very well what he meant when he spoke of Sif to Mummy Ti. Sif had not lived very long, but because she died many things had happened. Like so many beautiful creatures she was a victim of pollution — you could not think of angelfish and red pandas and butterflies, all lost and gone forever, without thinking of Sif. And yet, I saw, as Martin did, that the devastated Island, little by little, was becoming fertile again. A creeping vine with beadlike blue berries grew here and there in the decaying ash; ants scurried busily down the glassy lava; a spindly tree struggled to live in the shelter of a boulder. Survivors, plant or animal, made me think of my sister, too, for it was her death that made Henry and me and so many others begin to change the world.

At last we reached the menehune camp and sat down to rest. I could hear hushed voices and giggles from the depths of the earth. I gave the signal whistle Pig and I had used years before and in a little while, there was Pig, no higher than he used to be, but a good deal wider. He looked very much as his grandfather Axe had looked, earth-coloured and crumpled. No jeans, no, only a kilt of woven grass, and around his neck a coffee-tin lid on a plaited cord. We gave each other the nose-rub. I was so pleased to see him I shed a few tears.

'This is my brother,' I told Martin.

Pig was shy with the stranger; if Martin had said boo I think Pig would have twitched away amongst the rocks, never to be seen by either of us again. But I coaxed him to sit down and tell us how the menehune fared. Even before the eruption, they had burrowed more deeply, the way trolls ar ' the dark elves did when danger threatened in times gone by.

'But it hot down there,' said Pig. It seemed that even their ingenious ventilation systems sometimes failed.

I wondered if one day the menehune would build themselves a boat, pack up and sail off down some new star-path to find a safer home. I said as much to Pig, but he looked at me in wonder.

'No, no, Riko, no need for that.'

He had married, after all. His friend Mud, as we know, had two girls, and Pig married the elder one. Snail, her name is. She takes after her father and is a disagreeable box of dirty tricks. Still, Pig is fond of her. Amongst their children is a daughter, so perhaps the outlook is getting better for the menehune.

'Sure it getting better,' said Pig as we left. 'For menehune and all people in the world. I hear it in the air.'